"You are the most aggravating man—"

McCord cut her off. "Why? Because I organize my time better than you? Because I still find time for some form of relaxation?"

Celia put in succinctly, "I was wondering if you still frequented those places where Charriere gowns and chunky diamonds are common?"

Quick to divine her meaning, McCord smiled. "I do sometimes partner one of those enticing ladies." His quizzical blue eyes met her gaze. "Does that bother you?"

Oh, he really was insufferable! All six self-opinionated feet of him! And this in no way included his nauseating male conceit.

"Only in the sense—" Celia aimed at cutting him down to size before making a serene exit "—that their ideas of who and what make pleasant company must be quite different from mine!"

Desert Haven

by

ROUMELIA LANE

Harlequin Books

TORONTO • LONDON • LOS ANGELES • AMSTERDAM
SYDNEY • HAMBURG • PARIS • STOCKHOLM • ATHENS • TOKYO

Original hardcover edition published in 1981
by Mills & Boon Limited

ISBN 0-373-02485-1

Harlequin edition published July 1982

CHAPTER ONE

THE lobby of the Gulf Hotel was a-buzz with the conversation of that breed of humanity who hang around Middle East hotels. Architects, salesmen, women journalists, local executives; no one made a secret of their speciality and all were quenching the thirst of long hours waiting for some contact or other.

Celia was waiting for no one. She sipped diffidently near an archway, thankful for the slight circulation of air which wafted in from the hot, dusty street. Ever since her arrival in Bahrain the previous day she had been striving to come to terms with the dramatic change in climate. To her mind the general crush in the lobby made one barely aware of the air-conditioning.

But she was glad to be here, almost exhilarated to have got this far with her plan. Al Manamah, the capital of Bahrain, was just as her father had described it to her; if anything, more British than even he remembered. Apart from an occasional exotic touch in the decor, there was little to indicate that she was in the Middle East, and certainly the present company were as Westernised and amenable as any she would find at home. This was heartening.

It was only after another wayward glance around that the inclination to add a mild amendment to her summing up of the crowd made itself felt. She had described them as amenable, and so they were. All except one. He was tall, but not outstandingly so, nor was he particularly good-looking, yet she was conscious of a force in him that made her aware of—what was it—his disapproval of her?

She felt a fleeting resentment that there was one man in the room who guessed that she was not like the other

5

worldly, self-assured, never-put-a-foot-wrong types who decorated the lobby.

She decided to ignore him. She would be going out shortly anyway. She had only stopped by for a drink to give her the courage to begin the task she had set herself.

Once her mind reverted to the preliminary steps she must take she forgot the press in the lobby. There were lots of places she could start, of course, but all obvious ones and not for her. No, she must find her first lead alone. Celia more than anyone knew that her reasons for coming to Bahrain were, to say the least, a little bizarre.

She rose and as casually as possible made her way outdoors. The heat was like a blow on her thinly-clothed body. Knowing what she was about, she had put on her flimsiest of sundresses, a daffodil yellow with shoe-lace shoulder-straps for maximum cool.

She soon discovered that she had been hasty in condemning the air-conditioning of the hotel, but still it was good to be wandering through the streets of Al Manamah. She felt elated once again and curiously close to her dead father. How he had loved the East! He had never succeeded in shutting it out of his heart for all his long years later in England.

As she walked she looked around her a little uncertainly. She needed transport, but who in the general hubbub of weaving cyclists, trundling buses, darting urchins in tattered shirts and shorts, the traditional fez in most cases cocked cheekily, and plodding produce carts, could she approach?

She had purposely left the smart neighbourhood of the hotel behind, and though the balconied houses and shuttered buildings were as impersonal as she could have wished they were also unrevealing as to what kind of business went on behind. However, an idea did occur to her when she looked ahead and saw that the maze of streets she had followed was giving way to a stretch of open scrubland.

On a derelict patch was a sight that she would have called incongruous in this most Westernised of all the Arab states had the sand-laden breeze and hot blue sky not reminded her that she was indeed on the shores of the Persian Gulf. But it was the homely feel of the place which guided her footsteps unerringly to where the group of camels lazed, some on foot and others, legs folded under ragged humps, beside their owners.

Of course she didn't intend to adopt this mode of travel in her search, but as these camel-drivers were in the transport business they could no doubt tell her where she could find the four-wheeled kind.

In sentences carefully rehearsed for just such an occasion and with a natural feel for the tongue due to her father's long association with the language she stated her requirements in precise Arabic.

The reaction was both puzzling and disconcerting. She had simply asked where she could hire a car and she was confident her rendering had been impeccable, but by the look on the Bahrainis' faces she might have mouthed the foulest insult.

She quickly tried again, in case there should have been some lapse, and was alarmed to find herself, this time, encircled by the scowling, muttering group and nudged in the most unnerving manner.

Celia's cheeks grew hot. She might have been light-weight in appearance, but running through that slender frame was a thread of steely self-will, and after all, she had only asked a civil question. Unfortunately she was not sufficiently practised in the Arab language to put her point of view across, so all she could do was keep repeating that she wished to hire a car.

If she had tossed a hornets' nest in the midst of the drivers' camels the effect couldn't have been worse. With the blood-chilling feel of hands clutching at her she knew that the situation was getting frighteningly out of control. It was then that a sharp voice cut across the skir-

mish; an imperious '*Ibiird yadak*!' which had the effect
of parting the muttering mob like a whiplash.

Celia's glance flew along with everyone elses to the
sleek car that had stopped and the figure emerging. It
was the man whose eyes she had met across the lobby in
the Gulf Hotel. She hadn't liked him then and she didn't
like him now, as he came striding over with an expression on his face which said the scrape she had got herself
into was only what he might have expected. This was
verified by his opening words to her. 'I knew you were
heading for trouble the moment I saw you!'

Celia would have liked to make some withering reply
and as he pushed her towards his limousine she managed
to retort, 'What makes you think I'd add to it by
accepting a lift in a strange car?'

'Get in, and shut up.'

She had to admit that it seemed the wisest thing to do
under the circumstances, for although the man's presence had put a brake on the general anger it hadn't
cooled the tempers of the surly camel drivers, and feeling
herself almost wrenched from their grasp she didn't
hesitate to stumble into the plush interior, helped un-
ceremoniously by a pair of firm hands and an adequate
width of shoulder which held off the indignant mêlée.

Wasting no time on polite farewells, her tight-lipped
rescuer fell in beside her and drove off at speed, leaving
the unruly group shaking their fists in the road.

Celia had never pretended to understand their wrath,
and tremblingly incredulous she asked herself aloud,
'What did I do wrong?'

'Everything,' came the supercilious reply from the
wheel. 'Just like all the others who get bitten with this
lure of the East stuff, you choose nice cosy Bahrain because it's typically British. What you fail to realise is
that if you scratch beneath the surface of any Arab
country that used to be run by us you'll find that old
customs and habits remain.'

'Savagery included!' Celia unravelled herself from

where she had been pushed, quivering not only from shock but at the man's know-it-all attitude. 'What crime is there in asking to hire a car?' she snapped.

'Being new out here you wouldn't know,' she was told in a pitying, unsmiling way, 'that motor vehicles pose a threat to the camel-driver's trade and livelihood. In the old days the discovery of oil put many with no capital to invest in trucks out of business and those subsisting on the crumbs of the trade displayed their annoyance, sometimes with bullets. Now, with Bahrain's oil supplies running out, the old trouble has turned full circle. The camel owners see it as a return to the ancient ways of travel, so naturally they're not going to go out of their way to push the car-hire business.'

'Naturally,' Celia cooed from a heaving bosom. 'And they don't mind committing murder to emphasise their reluctance!'

Her choice retort made no impression on the granite-faced figure engaged in steering. He was busy with his own thoughts, and voicing them aloud he said, 'I followed you when you left the hotel. I knew you were going to come to grief sooner or later, starting out on your own.'

'So you said,' she purred, loathing his satisfied air.

He unnerved her by turning an arctic blue gaze her way and stating harshly, 'We don't find it funny extricating our own kind from foolish situations involving the locals.'

'Pardon me if I've been an embarrassment to you,' Celia said thinly.

'It happens all the time,' the wintry look returned to the road. 'Cheap air fares and trendy travel tours give the folk at home the idea that hopping over here is little different from sunning themselves on the beaches of Tangier. We're used to the gaffes some of them make, but we don't like it. It's not good for the British image out here.'

'It must be nice to be thoroughly weathered and above

making supid mistakes.' Celia eyed him with anything but admiration.

'It doesn't come from an afternoon sipping tea at a hotel lobby table, I can ensure you.'

Oh, he was insufferable! Of all the types to come to her aid in a sticky situation it had to be a grim, lecturing inured-in-the-East expatriate of hers!

Her heart recovering some of its normal rhythm after the disturbing ordeal, she noticed for the first time the views of rambling gardens and palm-screened villas sailing by. 'This is not the road to town,' she said sharply. 'Would you mind returning me to the hotel?'

'Later.' The man beside her drove on. 'I can't take you back like that.'

Celia had been too shaken to give a thought to her appearance, but now, following his glance, she saw that her dress had been torn at the bodice and a dangling shoulder strap showed a portion of creamy lace underslip. Colouring profusely, she clutched at the yellow remnants and to cover her confusion she murmured, 'Of course, I wouldn't want to embarrass you further by asking you to deliver me like this.'

'Nor would you want to advertise the fact,' he said with an exasperating curl to his lips, 'that just like a lot of other empty-headed tourists you drift straight off to the native quarter without taking the trouble to——'

'Now wait a minute! I've stood enough of your categorising, Mr. . . .'

'The name's McCord.'

And fitting too! Celia thought heatedly. His personality was about as flexible as stiffened lanyard. 'Unlike your superior opinion of newcomers to Bahrain,' she went on, 'I'm not here for the willy-nilly purpose of making a fool of myself. I happen to know a lot about this Arab state and my reasons for being here are . . . well . . .' Why did she have to hesitate just then? That was all he needed to treat her to another of his supercilious smiles, even though she finished firmly,

'Not that it's any of your business, but I do have a definite purpose for visiting Bahrain.'

'Don't tell me,' he drawled, 'you've come in search of the Moon God or to investigate the mysteries of Ramadan.'

Oh, he was impossible! She turned away impatiently, partly because she was guiltily aware that his suggestions were not that wide off the mark, and annoyingly too she had a feeling that he sensed it.

He brought the car to a stop at the edge of the desert and viewing the white wedding-cake structure as she alighted Celia carped, 'You didn't tell me we were going to pay a call on the local Sheikh!'

'This is my house,' he said, unamused. 'I have business interests in Bahrain.' He led the way into an interior which was cool and white and richly carpeted, sculptures with an Eastern flavour adding to the elegance and priceless objets d'art blending with the jewel-like colours underfoot.

Where arched windows looked out on to a hot, tawny nothingness Celia was left with the silent movement of pearl-finned fish swimming in a wall-length aquarium. In a moment her tight-lipped host had returned. 'First a drink, I think,' he said in an icy, businesslike way tinged with that familiar sarcastic gleam as he added, noting her trembling frame, 'Something stronger than tea this time, wouldn't you say?'

She had thought he would leave her again, but instead he came up to her and with one deft wrist movement ripped her dress from top to hem.

'*What are you doing?*' She turned on him with a fury that left him unaffected.

'It will save you having to disrobe in front of the servants,' he said calmly. 'Here, put this on.' He tossed her a silk robe he had brought from another room.

Feeling distinctly at a disadvantage standing there in her underslip, Celia didn't hesitate to do as he ordered, and especially as he wasted no time in pressing a button near his hand.

Before she had barely time to wrap the thing round her a soft-footed figure appeared in the doorway, and though his dark-skinned features were as impassive as one could have wished Celia hated her autocratic benefactor for putting her in the awkward position of having to stand there half buried in a dressing gown obviously belonging to the master of the house, and look as though she hadn't a care in the world.

A rapid spate of Arabic, followed by the daffodil remnants of her dress sailing his way, left the servant in no doubt, it seemed, as to his immediate duties. On his departure she was told, 'Quadi's pretty handy with a needle and thread. He also operates a sewing machine, so the chances are you won't know the difference when you get your dress back.'

Seething Celia took a step forward. 'I don't know what right you think you have——'

'Sit down before you fall down,' came the sardonic interruption.

It was true that since leaving the car the shock of her unfortunate encounter had attacked her limbs afresh, but she remained swayingly upright to fume, 'Just because I happen to have started off on the wrong foot on my first outing in Al Manamah it doesn't mean——'

'It's a pity you didn't think to ask some advice first,' he cut in yet again. 'It's fairly obvious to me,' he stood over her, wholly overbearing and objectionable, 'that someone like you wandering into the midst of a bunch of Bahraini camel-drivers and then having the nerve to ask about hiring a car would be like waving a red rag at a bull.'

Someone like her? Was he referring to her looks? Undoubtedly her fair hair and dove-grey eyes seemed to offend him.

In case that was it she countered, 'I don't see why I'm so different. When I arrived yesterday the market-place was full of European ladies shopping and managing on their own.'

'Sure, the frizzy-permed, dyed-in-the-wool ex-Army wives and so forth.'

Celia blinked at this reply. That couldn't be flattery, could it? Not coming from *him*? She didn't know whether to be more annoyed or not at his inference that she was not like the other travel-hardened members of her sex currently languishing with their husbands in Bahrain.

Under the circumstances and considering that, owing to his high-handed action concerning her dress, she could not now leave his house until it was returned to her, there seemed nothing for it but to seek a little support for her legs.

Ignoring his offer of assistance and feeling no match anymore for his sanctimonious remarks, clothed as she was in his ridiculously voluminous dressing gown, she dropped into one of the huge powder-puff armchairs and found the whole of her enveloped in such a fleecy cloud of comfort it was difficult not to give herself wholeheartedly to the experience.

While she was recovering some of her fight, though it wasn't easy with the sensuous luxury of the armchair sapping her will, the man who went by the name of McCord moved to a wall-side drinks cabinet. Gloweringly Celia eyed him at his task. He appeared to be completely at home in this land of robed Orientals. With dark hair and sun-weathered complexion he might have been one himself, except for those piercing blue eyes, of course, and an effortless Anglo-Saxon arrogance that no Arab could emulate.

In the silence of the room other sounds came to her, those of the indistinct tapping of a typewriter perhaps, an occasional footstep across tiled spaces and suggestion of distant activity. As though he read her thoughts her reluctant protector informed her, 'I do some of my office work on the premises. I'm in the refrigerating business.'

'That figures!' Celia said shrewishly. Whether her

spirited reference to his icy attitude had gone home she couldn't have said, but as she accepted the glass he offered she thought she saw—what was it—the glimmer of lazy appreciation in his eyes?

'I agree, there's unlimited scope for cooling measures in a country as hot at Bahrain,' he replied deliberately misinterpreting her remark. 'In my years at the job I've had no cause to complain. I've been asked to do everything from freezing the royal palace intake of fresh meat to arranging cold storage for imported medical supplies. At the moment I'm experimenting with an ice-rink in Manama, as we call it.'

'Shades of Western sophistication,' Celia commented idly.

'It's a sideline I've indulged in mainly through pressure from friends,' he shrugged. 'The Bahrainis are no different from their Arab neighbours when it comes to impressing the world with grand-scale modern amenities. If Saudi Arabia has an ice-rink then Kuwait has to have one. And if Kuwait has an ice-rink then Bahrain ...'

'Doesn't intend to be left out in the cold.'

'You've got it,' McCord almost smiled at her innocent pun but not quite. Instead he took a pull on his drink and finished drily, 'But I won't bore you with details of a business far removed from your ... er ... desert quest.'

It was uncanny, this foresight of his! Knowing that she had been a little crazy to come to Bahrain in pursuit of a dream, Celia said briskly, 'Not that far removed. I once got a silver medal for skating. I could probably show your Arab friends a thing or two ... and incidentally, how do they manage in local costume? It must be a bit restricting wobbling around in djellabahs and whatnot?'

'The people in these parts are pretty Westernised in dress—British influence again; though it hasn't reached the stage where girls can trip around in ballerina-length attire, but they cope . . .'

Celia had a feeling that they were marking time conversation-wise as though there were other more important things waiting to be said. She didn't think it was so much curiosity on McCord's part as to why she was in Bahrain as an imperious right to know. Because she was English he had taken it upon himself, high-handedly again, she thought, to put her straight as to what one did and didn't do in this tiny Arab state.

As she expected, after a moment or two he opened up the subject again with, 'It's not difficult to hire a car in Manama. What was the idea of wandering off the beaten track like that?'

'I had my reasons.' She lifted her chin.

'Reasons that may have cost you dear if I hadn't come along when I did,' he snapped.

She wanted to sound non-committal, but found herself saying instead, 'If you must know, I'm looking for someone.'

'Perhaps I can help.'

At this her lips curved wryly. 'I doubt it. This someone existed more than thirty years ago.'

There was no reply to that, she noticed with guilty satisfaction. He was foxed, and she couldn't blame him. It was a weird mission she had set herself.

He stood with his drink not far away. It was like him, Celia was discovering irritably to wait for further clues. She was prepared to let him wait—indefinitely. She had no wish to confide in him.

She had sipped quite a bit of the amber liquid he had poured into her glass, finding it bitter-sweet but strangely soothing. If it hadn't been for a peculiar lethargy which overtook her then she doubted whether she would have told him anything more. As it was, mellowed against her will by the drink and the cool restfulness of the room, she heard herself drifting into a reluctant explanation.

'My father was a government official out here in those days. He came to Bahrain in his teens and by the time he had risen to a decent level in his job he'd lost his heart to the East. Like most young men, single and content in his new way of life, he fell in love.

'Nevine was a dancing girl in a Manama night spot. But she was also beautiful and intelligent. They saw a lot of one another. It was a courtship made memorable by moonlight strolls through the date palm gardens and days spent on the Zallaq beach—and one that could only end one way. Nevine was terribly in love with my father.

'They planned to get married. Everything was arranged, but the wedding never took place. In those days matches of that kind were frowned upon, and my father was summoned home to England. His family were influential and certain strings were pulled which made it impossible for him to remain in Bahrain. In due course he married my mother, but he never forgot the Arab girl in Bahrain. I know that because my mother has been dead a long time and when two people are as close as my father and I were the old truths come out.'

Celia took a sip of her drink lost in her story by this time. 'I've never felt it was breaking faith with my mother's memory discussing Nevine. My father was a kind and considerate husband while she was alive, but he hasn't been able to hide the fact from me that Nevine was the love of his life; especially these last two years when he was bedridden for most of the time. To an invalid memories are all-important, and he loved most of all to reminisce with me about the past. Sometimes it was as though the intervening years had never been and that in thought his life in Bahrain and his happiness with Nevine were as close as if it had been yesterday.

'. . . I suppose it was when he died two months ago that I first got the idea to come out to Bahrain. Nevine is almost as much a part of me now as she was of my father. I felt I wanted to meet her, to get to know her—

the woman he had never ceased to love in all the years they were apart ... .'

There was a silence, a wholly disapproving one, then McCord set his glass down and bit out, 'Of all the sentimental . . .!'

'Claptrap?' Celia supplied demurely.

'Thanks for the adjective.' He glared at her. 'Are you trying to tell me that you've come all the way out here—and alone—to try to find this . . . this dancing girl?'

'She was a lot more than that.' Celia's chin went up. 'She was a star performer—and she came from a good family.'

'And what makes you think she'll be around now?'

'She would only be in her early fifties. Why shouldn't she be?'

'I don't suppose it's occurred to you that Bahrain is a pretty small place. She could have drifted off anywhere by this time; into neighbouring Kuwait maybe, or even Saudi Arabia.'

'No, she won't have done that,' Celia said with a distant look in her grey eyes. 'She's here in Bahrain. I feel it instinctively.' She saw his expression and stiffened. 'You can sneer if you like. I wouldn't expect you to understand. And it's precisely because Bahrain is such a small state—apart from its scattering of islands, no bigger than the Isle of Wight, my father used to say—that I don't think my search for Nevine will be too difficult.'

McCord looked at her for a long moment and obviously recalling the skirmish with the camel-drivers he pointed out, 'It still doesn't explain why you didn't order a car at the hotel desk and start your enquiries there.'

Celia fidgeted. 'I suppose I thought they'd . . .'

'Consider it an idiotic errand you'd come to Bahrain on?' he finished for her. 'And so do I. If I were you, Miss . . .'

'The name's Darwell,' she smiled thinly.

He bowed ironically. 'If I were you, Miss Darwell, I'd

pack my bags and return to England.'

'You may have business interests, but I don't think you own Bahrain, do you?' Her spirited comment was delivered smoothly.

'I can make it difficult for some fool English girl wandering around on an even zanier lovelorn mission.'

His harsh words made her react involuntarily. 'I don't suppose you can have any inkling of what this means to me?'

'It won't help trying to perpetuate your father's memory by searching out this . . . this Nevine.'

Was that what she was doing? She had to admit it would make her feel very close to her father if she could find and talk to Nevine.

Annoyed at the man's wisdom, she straightened. 'You can make it as difficult as you like, I intend to go through with it. And don't worry, I won't disgrace your Englishman's good name abroad by doing anything else foolish.'

'Do you want to bet?'

Oh, that supercilious look! Never had a man stirred her to such depths of resentment. She had only just met him, but she could cheerfully have hit him.

He took advantage of her being unable to frame a suitable reply to query, 'May I ask if you know any Arabic?'

'I've got a very good phrase book.'

He threw his glance to the ceiling, then nailed her again with it to probe, 'I take it you know the surname of this Nevine?'

'I . . . didn't think to ask my father.'

'Photograph?'

'There . . . was nothing in his effects.'

He let the breath escape through his teeth. 'So you don't know what she looks like and you don't know her name. That's great! It's likely to take you another thirty odd years to solve the mystery.'

'Time isn't an enemy to us all, Mr McCord.' She

countered his scorn with a show of confidence. 'I'm willing to bet Nevine is still beautiful today.'

'So all you have to do is look for a faceless, nameless, fading beauty among three hundred thousand inhabitants.'

'I can take all the discouragement you feel obliged to hand out,' she was then fired to reply. 'I wouldn't expect a hard-headed businessman to know anything about the affairs of the heart. But *I* don't intend to make heavy weather of it. For one thing, I happen to know that English is widely spoken in Bahrain, and as I see it, it's simply a matter of asking around.'

'You might do okay in Manama, but what if you have to go to outlying villages? Chances are you'll have to if nothing turns up in town.'

'I'll cope,' she said hardily. It was strange. Before she had clashed with this hardbitten countryman of hers she had been ready to admit that it was madness coming to Bahrain with the idea of searching out her father's old love. Now she was filled with a drive to prove that it was anything but that. Such were the things that opposition did to one; opposition in the shape of a big, clamped-jawed, disapproving Englishman, at any rate.

CHAPTER TWO

MCCORD added nothing to what he had already said, but Celia could almost hear him thinking, 'There's one born every minute!' as he looked at his watch.

It was yet another source of irritation to her to discover that he had timed the repairing of her dress almost to the second, for in the next moment the soft-footed servant reappeared and presented him with the daffodil yellow folds before discreetly departing again.

McCord held up the dress and went over it with his gaze in an aggravatingly leisurely manner. 'I do believe the old boy's pressed it too,' he tossed it her way. 'You're going to look decidedly better leaving the house than you did coming into it.'

Celia changed rapidly, tempted to throw his dressing gown back at him in the same way, but something about the icy spark in his eyes deterred her. She thought it changed to mockery as she opened her handbag, one frayed handle reminding her of her brush with the camel-drivers, to search for comb and powder compact. Perhaps it amused him in a coldly sardonic way to have a woman titivating herself in his wholly masculine domain.

Let him look! She combed her shoulder-length hair to some semblance of smoothness and patted her nose with a perfumed powder-puff. And defiantly too she retouched her lips with a flame-hued lipstick.

Everything replaced and her handbag hung lopsidedly over her wrist, she presumed McCord was waiting for her to leave, but contrary to moving towards the door he pressed another button close at hand and said without stirring, 'There's someone you should meet.'

Celia was hardly in the mood to prolong her stay.

The effects of the soothing liquor had long since cleared from her head and, wondering how she could have been so idiotic as to relate her trite story to this man of all people, she said, drily 'I think I've done enough socialising for one day.'

'I wasn't thinking in terms of entertainment' he returned crisply. 'Unless you consider the task you have set yourself falls into this category.'

Everyone seemed to jump to attention when he pushed those buttons, for in no time at all another figure not only appeared in the doorway, but this time walked respectfully into the room.

He was a little younger than his employer, being barely thirty perhaps, and Celia was struck by the contrasting warmth which seemed to fill the room with his arrival. His dark, luminous eyes took in the whole of her at a glance, returning to hover with lazy interest around her mouth. His Western dress didn't quite come up to the tailored perfection of McCord's tropical suit, but he was smartly attired in dark blue and though slight of frame there was a curious magnetism about him, an impish love of life, she felt, held sternly in check by that formal smile.

'Kamel, I want you to meet Miss Darwell.' It was McCord's voice which broke the spell of that look which passed between them, on the young Bahraini's side if not on Celia's; though she had an uncomfortable feeling that McCord had made his own lightning deduction of her reaction to the handsome young Arab. 'She's come to Bahrain to look someone up,' he went on, 'and it will be your job to give her whatever assistance she requires. You will pick her up promptly at nine in the mornings at the Gulf Hotel and deliver her there each day before dark. Is that clear?'

Celia couldn't believe her ears. The audacity of the man, interfering in her affairs this way! Who did he think he was, taking it upon himself to supply her with a guide! And at the precise hours *he* stated too!

She wanted to tell him so to his face, but that would have been insulting the young Arab, who was politely bowing her way, so she held her tongue.

'It's likely to be a prolonged search,' there was no mistaking those sanctimonious tones. 'Miss Darwell will give you all the details herself. Her safety will be your responsibility until she leaves Bahrain. Do you understand?'

'I will do as you wish, sir.' The reply was made in good English while those dark eyes roamed in Celia's direction again.

'Okay, Kamel, you can go now. And don't forget, Gulf Hotel, nine in the morning. You can use a company car.'

Dismissed in the peremptory way he had been summoned, Kamel was nevertheless sent about his business with a smile from McCord. To Celia it was totally unexpected. Hard and reserved, it was every bit in character with the rest of his granite features, yet she was fascinated by it. The shock that he could appear almost human left her with a wry feeling inside.

When they were alone again she wasted no time in letting him know that she was one, at least, who didn't intend to heel to his autocratic ways.

'Why did you do that?' she demanded hotly. 'I'm perfectly capable of making my own plans, thank you.'

'Kamel is one of several assistants I employ. I can spare him for as long as you want to keep up this fool quest.' He spoke as though the matter was closed, and stood aside for her to precede him. 'Shall we go?'

'Nothing would please me more!' It was the only scathing retort she could muster while brushing past him and even this, she felt, was lost on his tough exterior.

They made the drive back to the hotel in quivering silence—on Celia's part anyway. It was so humiliating to have to sit there and subject herself to his forceful handling of the situation. He ran people's lives, it seemed, in the same casual, steely way he was steering the car. She would dearly have loved to argue the point, but he gave her no opening. There was an unspoken air about him that defied the unsure—well, that was what he did to one—to contest his authority.

He came right in with her into the Gulf Hotel. In the lobby Celia said ungraciously, 'Please don't put yourself out for me. I *do* know my way from here.'

'I'm not doing you any favours,' he drawled in his tightlipped fashion. And looking around, 'I'm here to meet a lady.'

So! He was not too frosted over to appreciate the company of a woman once in while. For some reason his words struck a further note of discord within her and she was moved to aim at him, 'She has my sympathy, Mr McCord!'

'Call me McCord,' he smiled as though making sweeping concessions. 'Everyone does.'

She ignored his slight nod as he left her and swung away into the opposite direction, though it was not necessarily the right one for her. Little did he know that she had regarded him as plain *McCord* from the start. As far as she was concerned he was not the type to inspire anything other than the dehumanised approach. She doubted if he had ever *possessed* a christian name! And cared even less.

Celia was up bright and early the next morning. It was not that she was falling in with McCord's plans ... It was just that it did seem to her that the help of someone locally would make her task easier. To be truthful, she had had a go on her own the previous evening, but Manama at night-time was overwhelming and she hadn't known where to start in her search for Nevine. She would need assistance, she saw that now, and while she had no wish to be supplied with a guide out of McCord's camp, the man's integrity she was certain of, whereas if she hired a guide herself, who could say? Besides, she had a feeling that Kamel would be a lot more friendly than his employer.

Just how friendly she was soon to discover! His presence outside the hotel where he waited for her beside a practically dark saloon was eye-catching, to say the least. He was wearing a sand-coloured suit which emphasised his attractive olive-skinned features, and his smile as he greeted her was just about the warmest she had come across since her arrival in Bahrain.

'I am happy to be of service to you, Miss ...' he frowned humorously while showing her into the seat beside the driving wheel. 'But it is too beautiful a day to be on formal terms. If we are to be together so much we should start out as friends right away. Don't you agree?'

'Agreed,' she laughed at his easygoing audacity. 'I'm Celia, and I'm glad to know you, Kamel.'

'Celia,' he said it musically. 'I know the name. It has a Greek significance, has it not?'

'They do say!' she replied lightly, settling herself as he joined her behind the wheel.

'Heavenly ... that is the transposition in English, I believe,' he savoured the word with sensual lips while his liquid brown eyes amused themselves roaming her face. 'A charming meaning for a name, and one entirely befitting in your case, if I may say so.'

'You may.' Celia laughed again. What else could she do? But as his gaze continued to linger while the rest of the town traffic went about its business, she said, smiling back her embarrassment, 'Well, shall we go?'

'Ah yes!'

At this purposeful exclamation Celia was sure Kamel intended to get down to work. He discarded his jacket and confronted her with a decidedly less formal view of himself in open-necked sports shirt the whiteness of which did even more to enhance his attractive physique. Still purposeful, he started the car and told her, 'First I will take you to Isa Town, our beautiful garden city. Then I will show you El-Areen where——'

'But I haven't even explained about my search yet,'

she cut in to remind him.

'Well,' he shrugged philosophically, 'we will find a good spot where we can talk.'

A little helplessly Celia went along with the plan. She had had visions of making almost door-to-door enquiries in Manama concerning Nevine, and to be whizzing along country roads, albeit surrounded by interesting scenery, was not her idea of conducting a systematic search. Still, she supposed she had better let Kamel have his head to begin with. She had heard that in the East they took things more leisurely and she supposed it was not in an Arab's nature to get straight down to business.

She forgot some of her frustration when they came to Isa Town, a showpiece about eight miles out of Manama; the gateway to the town consisted of three impressive, futuristic archways, and after that it was gardens all the way. As she viewed the large concentration of new homes it occurred to Celia that Nevine, in later years, might have moved out here. She was excited at the thought, but there was little opportunity for making enquiries there and then. Kamel was giving her an offhand account of current development in the area, as though he considered he had certain duties to perform as a guide, and when this was over he promptly left the district for somewhere which was obviously closer to his heart.

The man-made oasis he parked beside some time later she had to admit was a charming spot—and it would serve nicely too, she decided firmly, for describing in detail the plans she had in mind.

'Kamel,' she said, dragging her gaze from the green of slender bamboo saplings and eucalyptus trees against the saphire sheen of lapping waters, 'don't you think I should tell you now why I'm here in Bahrain?'

'But of course! You must explain everything.' Her heart leapt at his enthusiasm, then sank again as he added, 'But first we will have lunch.'

'Lunch?' she gaped around. 'Out here?'

'Naturally I have come prepared.' He jumped out energetically on to the sand and proceeded to lay out a desert feast which was as incredible as it was inviting. There were cooked meat on little sticks, eggplant filled with aromatic herbs, grape-leaves stuffed with rice and mincemeat, white cheese, flat round bread, and dishes of figs, dates, olives and apricots.

Weakly Celia succumbed to the pleasures of eating. She hadn't allowed for taking time out to indulge themselves in this manner, in her itinerary, but she supposed they couldn't do what they had to do on empty stomachs. There were rugs to recline on and thirst-quenching liquids to go with the meal, and though she was impatient to make some start on tracking down Nevine she felt it would have been petty to throw cold water on Kamel's efforts.

He told her something about the wild-life sanctuary of El Areen while they ate, and the reserve which was dedicated to the preservation of rare Arabian species, but not with any great desire to impress her with the information. If anything he was inclined to be a little vague about their surroundings, concentrating more on creating a cosy atmosphere where they were camped beneath the spreading greenery of camphor trees.

Celia was grateful for the shade. She had donned cotton slacks and sleeveless blouse for the day's work, but even these were trying in the soaring temperatures of the Gulf. Her companion, like all Arabs, appeared not to notice the heat. She watched tapering horned oryx at a distance and striped gazelle nervously nibbling beside a fern-like copse. It was a far cry from how she had expected to be spending the first day of her quest; after all, there were no people here, people who might know or have heard of Nevine; just rare and timid animals. But the experience was not unpleasant, and the lapping waters of the oasis were decidedly soothing . . .

Kamel had a keen mind, obviously, or a man like

McCord wouldn't have employed him, but in the few hours she had known him Celia felt it was a condition he was not wont to put himself out about when away from the office. Like now, for instance. Lunch over, he had contrived to position himself next to her and on the intimate note he had fostered throughout their stay at this chosen spot he asked, 'What do you think of our country, Celia?'

'It's hot,' she blew the damp air from her brow, then viewing the pearly brilliance of the sky and exotic scenery she conceded laughingly, 'and exciting, I suppose.'

'You are right. I cannot deny that there is something about the air here in the East that quickens the blood.'

Because he was gazing deep into her eyes Celia said lightly, 'Have you had occasion to make comparisons?'

'But of course! I am a travelled man.' Kamel looked faintly hurt. 'I studied in Beirut with future British Ambassadors to the Middle East, and I have also spent some time in your country. Do you know what they say about Bahrain?' He was comparing the fairness of her hair against the dark cinnamon of his wrist. 'They call it the Welwyn of the Gulf.'

'Is that because of the uncommon amount of Britishers there are over here?' she asked steadily. 'Or because of the garden aspect of the place?'

'A little of both, I think,' he smiled before his eyes took on a luminous urgency. 'But there is no one in Bahrain who so resembles a cool flower in a raging climate. Your presence, like your name, my sweet Celia, is for us Bahrainis—heavenly.'

Celia floundered for a reply. At twenty-three she had learned how to handle persuasive young men. Before her father's illness she had attended the usual social gatherings, and her fair hair and fresh features had made her the inevitable quarry of the bolder members of the opposite sex. But Kamel! He worked faster than the speed of light!

Shaking herself from the hypnotic quality of his gaze,

she twinkled sternly, 'You may not know it, but the name Celia also signifies "one who commands", and I think it's time I got down to issuing a few. But first I'll tell you all about my reasons for being in your country.'

'Business! Business! Why does everyone always want to talk business?' he groaned.

'Contrary to common belief,' she teased, 'it's *that* that makes the world go round.'

Much against his will Kamel listened to all she had to say and when she had finished he didn't hesitate to give her his opinion of the matter. 'But that is a stupid idea!' He was petulantly incredulous. 'You cannot waste our time looking for some bag of an Arab woman when we are at the point of something so exciting in our lives.' He waved an arm. 'All this and much more can weave the memories for our future—the bathing delights of El Bakhor; the moonlight paths of Jamrah . . .'

'You're employed by Mr McCord, I believe, to do a working day, not to languish in lush tourist spots' Celia pointed out patiently. 'And please don't refer to Nevine in that way. She was quite a bit younger than my father and it's possible she may be still elegant and attractive.'

'But it is not Nevine who beckons across the barren stretches of my heart.'

Kamel could be impishly digressive and Celia had to work hard at pushing home her demands. 'We'll start in town. I think that will be the best place to begin our enquiries.'

'Very well,' Kamel became brisk too. 'We will return to Manama, and I shall be a slave to your wishes. No house or business will escape the purge of our enquiries, but I too have my conditions. After dark is my own time and I shall make a supper reservation for two at the Moon Guest restaurant. We will take up there the quest you force me to abandon now . . . the linking of hearts.'

It was blackmail in the subtly charming, Eastern tradition, and Celia was mildly apprehensive about the 'linking of hearts' bit, but, worriedly aware that she was now in her third day in Bahrain with only limited resources in her purse, she accepted with a lighthearted 'Done!' and fell to helping him to pack away the picnic things. Any start was better than none.

Kamel was as good as his word. He worked with a conscientiousness that Celia felt any man of McCord's would, approaching owners in shops and town houses and places of entertainment with the courteous affability of his race, and lapsing into fiery Arabic and abuse when dealing with the slow-witted, also a trait in his kind.

Celia possessed no likeness of Nevine, but she did carry a photograph of her father, taken as a young man when he had worked in Bahrain. She showed this around expectantly at first but after much foot slogging and hovering in the background listening to negative responses, her optimism was replaced by acute disappointment, and she began to see that the thing she had set her heart on was going to be no easy task.

No one had heard of any person going by the name of Nevine. Many suggested that it might have been a stage name the dancer had adopted for her profession, but all proffered blank faces and empty-handed gestures. Even the elderly had no recollection of such a woman in their midst.

When the town became lit by the plum-coloured glow of dusk Celia was more than ready to call it a day, and after a refreshing shower in her hotel room and a change of clothes she found she was not averse at all to dining out with Kamel. Work, no matter how exciting in some cases, could pall, she had discovered, if one didn't give it a rest.

She hadn't packed an extensive wardrobe for the simple fact that she didn't possess one, but her dreams of finding Nevine had prompted her to want to look her best for the occasion, so her favourite garments had accompanied her on this trip. One was a summer dress in creamy seersucker which she was wearing now. She pinned on a diamanté brooch to give it an evening touch and with similar winking lights showing when the thick sweep of honey-pale hair revealed her earlobes, she considered the effect wasn't too bad.

Kamel was waiting for her in the lobby of the hotel. It was thickly populated as usual, and as she was crossing the spaces to meet him she caught sight of McCord in with the wandering traffic of guests. He had seen her, she noticed—well, that was possibly an understatement, his eyes were fixed on her as she moved before him as though he expected her, at any moment, to commit another faux-pas. She met his gaze somewhat defiantly in passing. He was bound to see her meet up with Kamel, of course, but so what? This was Kamel's free time, and he wasn't boss over *that*, was he?

The Moon Guest Hotel housed a restaurant that was both intimate and exclusive. The Chinese cuisine and Korean royal food were an experience for Celia, but neither was as devastating as Kamel's burning presence. The longing to participate in something other than knocking on street doors and confronting blank faces had made her forget the bulldozing charms of her Arab assistant.

His attentiveness during the meal would have been embarrassing if she had taken it seriously. But for all her lightheartedness little whispers of doubt kept coming to plague her as to the wisdom of agreeing to spend the evening with him. He could be unnervingly possessive, she was noticing, and his 'linking of hearts' talk of earlier, and 'weaving the memories for our future', caused her some concern behind her smile.

When they got up to leave after the meal, his arm turned quite naturally about her waist and he told her close to her ear, 'Before we go, I have a little surprise for you. Come,' he indicated the way through a beaded curtain.

Approaching displays of jewellery and gifts along a carpeted corridor of the hotel, Celia was horrified to discover that Kamel intended to buy her a trinket. Slant-eyed girls showed her trays of rings and pendants in imperial jade and coral brought specially from the Far East, and when her Arab companion placed a necklace around her throat she gasped, 'Oh no, Kamel! I hardly know you.'

'What is time, measured in the earthly way?' Those liquid dark eyes met hers. 'You and I have lived a thousand years since meeting. It is certainly the moment to show my appreciation for the gift that Allah has delivered into my arms.'

She wasn't in his arms, nor had she any intention of ending up there, but her polite refusal to accept a trinket from him met with the same charming disregard with which he viewed all her negative responses. In the end she settled for a simple pendant affair of mystic Oriental design which he took great pleasure in fastening about her neck.

Out in the warm, charged air of night-time in the Gulf she knew she was going to have to stand firm, and taking a breezy attitude she said, 'Well, it's back to the hotel now, Kamel. We mustn't forget we have an early start to make in the morning, and I am rather tired.'

'But you know nothing of Manama by night!' He was obviously put out at her rapid rounding off of the evening. 'We have discothèques and——'

'I've seen enough of it by day,' she replied wryly. 'Now are you going to drive me back or shall I take a taxi?'

He gave in peevishly, and later, alighting outside the entrance to the Gulf Hotel, Celia was smitten sufficiently by his glum features to offer, 'Thank you for a perfect evening, Kamel, and I do appreciate the pendant—it's lovely. I hope we'll have another good day work-wise tomorrow.'

'Of course I shall wait for you at the appointed hour,'

he said aloofly before driving off.

Despite this polite assurance she half expected to see
no Kamel or a very disgruntled one the next morning.
But contrary to her expectations he greeted her beside
the car with his glowing smile, and radiating his usual
warmth and energy; though energy for what? she asked
herself with a sinking feeling noting picnic and beach
gear as she got into the car. 'First we will go to Yafamas
for morning coffee,' he told her gaily, 'then to the beach
at Ras-al-Kar. It is a superb day for a swim, there is a
cooling *shamal* blowing and——'

'But I don't *want* to swim,' Celia cut across his suggestions firmly. 'I want to find Nevine.'

'So! We have eight whole hours.' He was complacent.
'And if you wish we can ask around along the way.'

'I want to do more than that, Kamel. I want to follow
up any line of enquiry which may reveal Nevine's
whereabouts,' Celia said patiently.

'That too,' he shrugged flexibly. 'But as it is a tedious
occupation conversing with the rabble about some
frayed Arab ... matron, why should we not enjoy a
swim for our labours?'

The way he put it there was little footing for argument and Celia was bound to go along with his bargaining tactics ... that day and the ones that followed.
Once she got the hang of falling in with his plans to
overwhelm her with his company and the sights of the
island in return for his assistance in the matter of
Nevine, comparative peace reigned. But it was an uneasy
peace where Celia was concerned.

She couldn't complain of any reluctance on Kamel's
part to make a thorough search for the woman who
had been so much a part of her father's life thirty years
before. Besides traversing the corridors of smart seaside
apartments and palmshaded communal residences they
combed the countryside and outlying villages, stopping
at hamlets to knock on decrepit doors and waylaying
camel and donkey traffic to enquire of their owners.

But balancing with this were the languorous afternoons they spent beside the blue waters of the Gulf and in the garden pools of sophisticated Bahrain hotels, time enough to foster an ever-increasing intimacy between them which she was helpless to counteract.

Though she drew the line at seeing Kamel every evening, pressure in the form of some extra zest on his part in their joint search made her feel obliged to show her gratitude with an occasional supper together; concessions which something told her were far from wise.

She also had McCord at the back of her mind. She had seen him in the hotel again on another occasion, and it would have to be when she was loaded up with beach bag and bathing gear on her way to meet Kamel. She recalled his terse statement that he had not been thinking in terms of entertainment when offering her the services of a guide, and she was reminded rather guiltily that it was McCord who was paying Kamel's wages.

She couldn't help wondering too, at times, about McCord's mysterious lady friend. He was often to be seen in the lobby of the Gulf hotel, but so far she had spotted no feminine figure at his side. Where did he keep her?

But dominating her consciousness most of the time was the glum fact that she was no nearer to finding Nevine now than she had been at the start. Of course there had been moments when her hopes had soared; when it had happened that someone bearing the same name was known to be residing in some out-of-the-way village or backwater section of the town. But each time it had turned out to be a false trail with the woman in question being some stallholder who had worked at nothing else since childhood or a farming type whose whole life had been the land she and her husband tilled.

The days were flying by; a state of affairs that Celia was all too aware of. She was running up a bill at the hotel which threatened to take the last of her reserves.

Coupled with Kamel's ever-increasing possessiveness where she was concerned, things were, to say the least getting out of hand. The moment she knew that she would have to forget her dream of finding Nevine and return to England came when they had just left a hamlet of cubic dwellings with the usual negative results and were driving back to the more populated sections of the island. Palm trees rose in misty splendour beside damply irrigated lush green farm strips and the idea of never knowing the woman whom her father had idolised filled Celia with an intense sadness. But it had been a wild scheme anyway and she should have known that the chances of success were remote.

She chose a relaxed period when they were sipping mango juice at a beachside table to tell Kamel that she was abandoning the search. He made no attempt to hide his pleasure. 'Good!' he beamed. 'Now we can think solely about ourselves.'

'But, Kamel, you don't understand' she explained wearily. 'I came to Bahrain only for a limited stay. Now that time is up I have no choice but to return to England.'

'You have one other choice,' he took her hand. 'Celia, my heavenly Celia, you must know by now that I want to make you my wife.'

'Kamel!' She was staggered, though she fought hard not to show it. 'We've only just met. A fortnight together doing guided tours of Bahrain is not the basis for the kind of partnership you suggest.'

'Nevertheless you shall be my first wife,' he said stubbornly.

First wife! Celia would have reviewed the whole thing with humour if Kamel had not been so petulantly serious. She saw the burning desire in his eyes and wondered if all Arabs worked on making such lightning conquests.

All along she had sensed that her guide was getting a charming fixation about her, but she had not forseen in her farewell speech the possibility of having to make a refusal of marriage. Nor was it as simple as that. As Kamel was a man who obviously didn't like to be crossed she could see she was going to have to oppose the idea with everything she possessed.

The arguments she offered lightly at first and then otherwise had no effect on him. So in the end she told him gently but firmly that she would be catching the plane home the following day, and that in time he would find someone who would make him a much better wife than she would.

It did seem then that her words had got through. 'Very well,' he gave a shrug, his gaze somewhat hooded. 'But before you leave I think there is one more possibility we should try concerning this dancing girl of the past.'

Celia couldn't believe that he was seeing sense at last, but happily this appeared to be the case. A little in wonder, as he had never offered suggestions of this sort before, she said, 'Somewhere where we might find Nevine? But if you think there's a chance why haven't you mentioned it earlier?'

'It has only just come into my head,' he shrugged again, and then with growing enthusiasm, 'But I am sure there is every reason to believe that this time we may be lucky.'

His words triggered off a new excitement in Celia. It had been known before to hunt and hunt for something and then find it under one's nose. And anywhere in the small state of Bahrain that could happen, couldn't it? Her hopes soared unaccountably. It might still be possible to meet and talk with Nevine after all before she had to leave for England. It could be that having got the nonsense of his proposal out of his mind Kamel was thinking clearly for the first time.

Increasingly optimistic, she asked, 'But where is this place?'

'Out in the desert, somewhere we have never thought

of looking, and I think we should go there right away.'

Celia was a little taken aback at Kamel's sudden zest for work, but she went along with him happily enough to the car, her mind re-inspired conjuring up pictures of a gentle-featured woman who had once been the young Arab girl of her father's heart.

They drove for some time leaving the beaches of Zallaq behind and making for an area which appeared to be devoid of all living matter, going by the look of the yellow haze beyond the windscreen. But surprisingly, Celia was to discover, there was one habitation in all these barren miles of dusty desert; a cubic dwelling of sorts with onion-shaped archways leading to other buildings, and a minaret and palm trees giving it the look of a traveller's rest.

What was odder still to Celia, for the oasis had a deserted air, was that Kamel drove straight into the sand-strewn courtyard and alighting helped her rapidly from her seat. Hesitatingly she got out and looked about her. 'You can't mean here?' she was frowningly incredulous. 'The place looks derelict . . .'

'That's the impression one gets,' he took her arm. 'But I do happen to know of a recluse staying here.'

'A recluse?' Celia's heart lifted suddenly. She looked at Kamel expectantly.

'A recluse,' he nodded mysteriously, 'who is known to have been an entertainer in her time.'

Celia was spurred into action. Could it be? Was Nevine, love-lost like her father, living out her life here, lonely and forgotten?—Or so she thought.

Celia almost ran with Kamel to the doorway he indicated. Fleetingly it struck her as strange that he seemed to know his way around. And when he produced a key to the door her whirling senses, thinking only of the prospective meeting with Nevine, were too lit up with excited anticipation to register the fact.

She walked into a low-ceilinged room. Vast and ornately furnished in true Eastern style, it wore an air of outdated luxury. The tasselled hangings, sumptuous sofas, carpets and velvet cushions exuded the musky odour of age, and rich mosaics and lacework drapes had yellowed with time.

Celia had time to notice all this while she waited, keyed up, for someone to appear at their arrival. But all she heard was the slam of the door at her back. At first she thought it was a trick of the breeze which had sculptured the sand-drifts in the courtyard, but when she heard the turn of the key in the lock, puzzlement took the place of her glowing anticipation and she called, 'Kamel! What are you doing? Do you realise you've locked me in?'

His voice came back, soft and caressing close to the door. 'That was my intention, my heavenly Celia. And you will stay locked in until you agree to become my wife.'

Celia listened horror-stricken. 'You mean—there's no Nevine in this place?—It was all a trick just to get me here?'

'I had to think of something.' His tones were peevishly apologetic. 'I decided from the first moment I saw you that I wanted you for my wife. You have upset all my plans by refusing my wish, but I think it will be simply a matter of time before you change your mind.'

'Kamel!' She beat in a frightened way on the door. 'You're not going to leave me here? You can't! I have to return to England tomorrow . . . and besides, it won't do you any good. You must see the idea of a marriage between us after so little time is rid——'

'I will return in a few days,' the voice came from further away. 'We will see then how strongly you resist my desires to make you my betrothed.'

'A few days?' Celia hammered, panic-stricken. 'Kamel! Let me out at once! Stop this stupid game, do you hear? Kamel! . . . Kamel?'

The only reply this time was the sound of the car starting up, and soon her cries and beatings upon the door were drowned in its noisy departure. When she listened again the rumble of the engine was fading fast in the distance, leaving her surrounded by an eerie and breeze-whining silence.

Half angry and half laughing at the craziness of the situation, Celia wandered into the room and found a seat. But it had ceased to be funny when the arched windows began to show the blue-black night of the desert and Kamel still hadn't returned.

Exhausted, she curled up as best she could on one of the sofas, reminded, for some inexplicable reason in all this faded luxury, of the after-scent of Turkish Delight. But the furtive scufflings around the corners of the room doused any humour she might have felt at the thought and she spent a sleepless night listening to these and other unnerving sounds around the desert outpost.

Dawn came and the morning passed with her pacing the room in between frantic bouts of looking for a means of escape, all of which proved fruitless. Kamel had known what he was doing imprisoning her here. Every entrance she explored outside her immediate surroundings was sealed and the room, despite its elegant trappings of the past, had the barred-in feel of a fortress.

It was just after lunch-time by her watch when she heard the heartening sound of a car approaching. So Kamel had relented and returned! Or maybe he thought she had already changed her mind. Well, she wouldn't be such a fool as to let him believe any different until she was well clear of this place. Conjuring up in her mind the sweet replies she would give him, she rushed to the windows, but they overlooked the rear of the courtyard and she could see nothing. All she could rely on was her hearing, and something told her that the vehicle that was fast approaching was not the one she was used to hearing Kamel drive her around in. The rhythm of the engine was different, for one thing, and suddenly she was filled with a new and blood-chilling fright. What business other than questionable could anyone have in a ghost-town place like this?

Instead of rushing to the door as the car came to an abrupt stop in the courtyard, she backed away. And at the sound of footsteps making straight for the door, *her door*, she paled. *That* certainly wasn't Kamel's soft-shoed tread.

The knob turned right and then left. She watched it hypnotised. Would the caller go away? She stood transfixed, then jumped back a step or two as some great weight was hurled against the door. It was a strongly fabricated structure, but it soon began to give against the powerful force at the other side.

Her blood running cold, Celia knew she ought to *move*; run, hide, anything but just stand there. Yet stand there she did, rooted with horrified fascination as the door began to splinter before her eyes. The sound of laboured breathing came to her ears. An extra, super-human effort and the door cracked before her and fell away to reveal in its opening an awry and familiar figure.

McCord looked at her in that disapproving way of his, squared himself in the doorway and heaved, 'I thought I'd find you here.'

CHAPTER THREE

STRUGGLING to appear unaffected by his appearance, Celia replied flippantly, 'Your powers of perception are amazing. Given one unlocked door on these premises and you could have been wrong.'

'Yes, it's a pretty neat stronghold,' McCord acknowledged, brushing himself off. 'And trust you to end up stuck in the middle of it.'

'Well, believe me, I'm not enjoying the experience!' Celia thought she would get that point home. More relieved than she cared to admit at seeing McCord, she asked crossly, 'How did you know I was here?'

'Simple deduction.' He lifted sizeable shoulders clothed in dust-powdered desert garb. 'I noticed that Kamel was back at his desk as usual this morning. But I learned at the hotel that you hadn't checked out.'

'So naturally I was bound to be locked and barred away, in some distant desert retreat,' Celia reasoned satirically.

'That's just about it in Kamel's case.' McCord was unamused. 'It's not the first time he's used this place to try to weaken the opposition where a girl's concerned. Although I employ some of the keenest brains among the local Arab population they do at times tend to revert back to nature, and Kamel has had designs more than once in starting up his own harem here at Al Minbah.'

Feeling more foolish than she cared to show, Celia fumed, 'Well, you might have told me!'

'I thought you would have the good sense to avoid that kind of entanglement,' he snapped back.

'Avoid it?' Celia was stormily incredulous. 'If I'd ridden around in the car trunk all the time I couldn't have escaped Kamel's wooing ways. He has a kind of demolishing approach, as you've probably noticed.'

'As I remember it,' McCord's expression was cynical, 'you were a long way from riding in the car boot. In fact I'd say Kamel was half-way there, with the kind of encouragement you gave him.'

Encouragement! Oh, why was it that whenever she met this man her fingers always itched to come into forceful contact with those self-important, hardbitten features?

Containing her fury, she said with flashing-eyed mockery, 'It would be interesting to know how *you* would have handled the situation had it been a seductive female in the driving seat!'

He looked at her, his blue eyes enigmatically self-indulgent, as he replied, 'I hardly think that has any relevance in the argument, do you?' and she could have kicked herself for giving him the opportunity of demonstrating, once again, his male superiority.

While she was thinking, against her will, about his mysterious lady friend at the Gulf Hotel he added with his usual asperity, 'And as you appear to be unharmed and little the worse for the experience I suggest we get out of here.'

He stood aside for her to step over the remnants of the battered down door, and feeling considerably light-headed after the eruptive exchanges with her formidable rescuer—his extracting her from sticky situations was becoming a habit, and oh, how he loved to labour her shortcomings!—Celia made her way unsteadily into the courtyard.

Nothing would have induced her to display the cosy feeling of security which enveloped her in the haven-like interior of McCord's car. She waited until they were speeding away from Al Minbah before putting in smoothly, 'It may sound a silly question, but why didn't you confront Kamel with what you had obviously guessed about me, and ask him for the key to my prison?'

'It wouldn't have done any good,' came the level reply. 'He would have denied the whole thing and probably thrown the key away to detach himself from the matter. The oasis, which was famous in the days before the oil boom, belongs to his family. In his mind you could have become just another part of the past until he felt sufficiently mollified to come and look you up.'

Celia shuddered. She really was glad now that McCord had burst the door in. She had been a lot more frightened than she had let herself believe, and her instincts had proved correct, it seemed. Since she had neither eaten nor slept for more than twenty-four hours it didn't bear thinking about how much longer she would have had to remain in this piteous state had it been left to Kamel. Spent as she was, she couldn't resist a wry smile at the so-called 'affection' of some Arabs.

She hadn't meant to demonstrate further her incompetence where McCord was concerned by collapsing into a deep sleep on the ride back. But the bright outdoors, the steadily drumming rhythm of the car wheels over rough ground, and the barren landscape, all acted like a drug on the mind. And such was her drained state that she never remembered dropping off. Nor had she the remotest intention of letting her head fall to rest on a comfortably-padded shoulder, and horror of horrors, she stirred at one point to discover that she had actually done this. But the deep bliss of this longed-for dreamless state was so all-encompassing she had no real will-power to fight her anti-McCord feelings . . . not for the moment at any rate.

Had she known what was coming when the car stopped she might have made some effort to revive. But there again, perhaps she was too wrapped up in the euphoria of sleep to care much when McCord began to shovel her up in his arms; though she did stir enough to protest dopily, 'Where are we? Oh no, not the Sheikh's palace again!'

'His title now is Emir, he was promoted on independence,' McCord corrected her, making for the indoors. 'And though it may look roomy I can assure you El Zommorro in no way compares with the royal abode.'

Even so, it was a beautiful house, Celia had to admit, if only from what she remembered of it on her last visit. A blur of rose gardens passed her sleepy vision, then she was aware of a whispered commotion in the cool interior as servants were sent on hurriedly ahead.

A staunchly independent type, she couldn't understand this powerful feeling of lethargy; a warm contentment to stay where she was nestled against a hard chest. Distantly in her mind she could hear the solid rhythm of a heartbeat. She was lulled again into oblivion by its comforting thud, surfacing momentarily when her head touched cool pillows, and then only to give a blissful sigh.

When she awoke the sky beyond the windows was aglow with the lilac and amber suffusion of dusk. She raised herself, noticing how the light filled the room with rose-violet tints; a room richly but moderately furnished to give a feeling of airiness.

Over a white carpet, realising that her shoes had been removed, she explored and discovered an adjoining bathroom suite; a sight that had never looked so inviting to her dust-rimmed eyes. it was good too, in the flower-shaped porcelain bath, to soak away all traces of the musty-smelling makebelieve harem where she had been imprisoned for so long. But when she was dressed again, and reasonably groomed, the pale face staring back at her from the mirror was not too heartening a sight for all her efforts.

A reeling sensation reminded her that she had not eaten since lunch-time the previous day. Though she had been too exhausted earlier to think of food, now she realised that she was in urgent need of some kind of sustenance.

The house was silent as though enveloped in the hush of approaching darkness. There was no sound now of the muted office-like atmosphere she had divined on her last visit. Outside her room she followed tiled corridors dimly lit to a curving stairway. Below, doors ajar on all sides showed interiors tastefully lit in a subdued way. Choosing the most open one of these, where slightly more illumination spilled out into the hallway, Celia saw at once that her guess had been correct.

McCord was leisurely pulling on a cigarette in an armchair lit by a pool of lamplight, a sheaf of what appeared to be business papers on hand. He rose when he caught sight of her and, confronted by the length and breadth of him in tailored evening wear as opposed to the desert garb of earlier, she became stiff again and impatient with her lapses of the afternoon.

'I'm grateful for your hospitality,' she offered truculently. 'But I would have preferred you to drop me back at the hotel.'

'Drop might have been the operative word,' he said, observing her drily.

Meaning to say that she would have fallen flat on her face in the lobby from fatigue, no doubt.

'Oh, of course!' She made a show of recollecting a previous conversation. 'We have to remember not to let the side down, don't we?' And recalling how he had transported her in his arms to the room she had woken up in, she added, 'It's amazing the lengths some people will go to, to keep up the image.'

'Isn't it,' he replied noncommittally.

Celia would dearly have liked a chair to support her rubbery legs, but as McCord didn't offer her one she drifted with as much dignity as she could muster to the nearest one and sank down, suppressing an exclamation of relief.

The room, she noticed, was not quite on the grand

scale of the others she had seen. Furnished in a more intimate style it was probably a dining room for a table, set in this instance for two, under the golden glow of a low chandelier, was its main feature.

McCord reached to press one of the inevitable buttons and as savoury-smelling dishes appeared in the hands of shadowy assistants he said, 'You'd better get yourself over to the table while you're still upright. You're not exactly a heavy weight to haul around, but I don't fancy having to cart you off to bed a second time—not on an empty stomach.'

Wobbling to a chair which he held for her beside the table, she flashed him a facetious look. 'I'd hate you to miss dinner for me!'

It was impossible to remain wooden with all this delicious food laid out, though she did make a feeble attempt while feverishly helping herself with the remark, 'There was really no need to extend your hospitality to include feeding me. I could have managed quite well at the hotel.'

'What happened at Al Minbah is a company matter,' McCord said, filling her glass and his own with a local wine. 'The unpleasant adventure you got yourself mixed up in involved an employee. As Kamel is my concern it's up to me to make amends for the damage that has been done. Eat.'

Since he put it like that Celia had really no more reservations about digging in. He jolly well owed her some compensation after what she had been through at the hands of his marriage-crazy guide, and she intended to make the most of it.

In her undernourished condition the meal was heaven. Combining European tastes with a dash of Arabic flavouring here and there, every dish sampled was a gastronomic experience. And there were the usual displays of dates and fruit and Turkish Delight vying with pastry-thin fibres baked with nuts and cream or raisin cake steeped in milk, for sweet.

McCord finished long before Celia did, and while she was busy peeling her second tangerine he sat back in his chair and asked, 'How's the search going for Nevine?'

Aglow now and in a much pleasanter frame of mind, she answered with a sigh, 'Not good, I'm afraid. Kamel and I have combed the whole of Bahrain—that is, Awal, I think you call this main island—without so much as turning up a clue. It's as though she never existed.'

'What about the smaller islands, Muharraq, and the Hawars?'

'We've had extensive enquiries made in those regions, with much the same results.'

'Even so, it wouldn't hurt to go there personally and do some looking around.' McCord was thoughtful. 'Jalal, a young assistant of mine, is a native of the Hawar Islands . . .'

Celia looked at him and exclaimed with feeling, 'Oh no! Not one of your Arab guides again!'

At the stricken note in her voice he reconsidered and said with a tight grin, 'No, perhaps not.'

He asked for coffee to be served through an adjoining doorway, and preceding him, Celia found herself in a sheltered balconied affair lush with the tropical growth of potted palms, climbing vines and sweet-smelling plants.

The furniture was garden-like and the lighting hidden amongst the greenery; not that one needed light with a view like this, Celia mused. There were no gardens at this side of the house, just the yawning emptiness of the desert. But what an emptiness! Stars filled a sky which swept low to distant horizons, spangling the night with a mystic awareness of the heavens and their time-lessness.

As though to bring her back to earth McCord said, 'The glow you can see is from the lights and oil flares at the Dahran oilfield. Bahrain,' he went on, 'is fortunate in possessing inland springs which bubble up in the most unlikely places. I chose this site for the house because it has one of the best springs of drinking water on the island.'

'I might have known it wasn't picked for its romantic location,' Celia replied drily.

Nevertheless it was romantic. The peach glow of the oilfields had a remote and faraway glamour and across the barren wastes wafted the warm scents of the Gulf waters and the whispered flurry of night insects.

Unexplainably Celia was filled with a curious desire to flee. Her eagerness to take in the view had brought her to the balustraded edge and though the balcony was by no means cramped the shadowy bulk of McCord close behind her had a stifling effect. She had a feeling that this was one of his favourite retreats at El Zommorro; here where all this thriving greenery—and his own virile presence, she couldn't help adding—cocked a snook at the impotency of the desert.

She also reminded herself that he had rested and dined her solely to compensate for the trouble caused by one of his employees, so it would not be in keeping to go weak-kneed at her surroundings.

With this thought in mind she went briskly to the glass-topped table to pour, and for the next ten minutes or so they sat in silence over coffee.

McCord was the first to rise. Realising that it was time to go, Celia discovered that the restlessness she had experienced earlier had mellowed to an odd reluctance to stir. She was conscious of a great peace here, a magic, one might almost say, which in a way helped her to understand her father's lifelong affinity with the East and Bahrain. And in turn she knew a tremendous melancholy at the thought of Nevine, who had been so close to him, unfound and unknown to her out there.

Apart from that brief discussion during dinner concerning the search for her, nothing more had been said on the subject of the dancing girl of the past. But when they were in the car on the way back to Manama

McCord let it be known that he had had an idea.

'I'm invited to a dinner party over at Rifaa tomorrow night,' he drawled. 'It's where the aristocracy reside. If you fancied coming along you could do some discreet probing among the guests.'

'For Nevine?' Celia sat up straighter.

He shrugged. 'You said she came from a good class family. It was just a thought.'

'Why, yes, I'm sure she was well born, despite the profession she chose,' Celia pondered eagerly. 'Though one can't say whether she's had to suffer any kind of repercussions in later life, because of it.'

'Have your enquiries covered that stratum of society?' McCord asked.

'As far as it was possible to do.' She looked wry. 'The kind of gatherings you mention are not that easy to gain access to in Bahrain.'

'That's why I suggested it.' McCord swung the wheel, his eyes on the road.

Equally detached now, she considered his words and asked, 'Wouldn't I be gatecrashing?'

'Not if you come with me. I'll pick you up at five tomorrow afternoon.'

She crooked an eyebrow. 'Didn't you say *dinner* party?'

'That comes later,' he replied non-committally. 'First we'll have to go through the usual Eastern ritual, which could prove useful for you.'

In what way Celia couldn't be sure, so she thought it best to wait and see. But she was keyed up at the prospect. As her glance strayed towards the outdoors the familiar surge of glowing anticipation rose within her. Another chance! Another possibility of finding Nevine!

They were fast leaving the desert behind and in contrast to its sombre magnificence Manama flaunted like a tawdry woman of the night. There was glamour here of a hardened kind in the strands of twinkling lights, in the flashing neon signs at the tops of high-rise buildings, and the headlights glitter of cars on the dual carriageway beside the sea.

At the Gulf Hotel Celia noticed how McCord accompanied her indoors, and it occurred to her then to remark obtusely before he left her, 'Are you sure I won't be making myself unpopular with ... er ... your other friends at the hotel if I accompany you tomorrow evening?'

He said with parting irony, 'Don't worry, I'll arrange it.'

In her hotel room around four the following afternoon Celia floundered in a certain amount of indecision. She was quite decided that she wanted to go to the dinner party, but of her escort for the outing she was not so sure. McCord needled her in a way she couldn't explain. He was always finding fault with her behaviour in his precious adopted country, and as an expatriate she fell far short of his ideals; mainly because since her arrival he had had to fish her out of one compromising situation after another. It was no good trying to explain to him that fate seemed to be taking a wicked delight in landing her in these tight spots. He put it all down to featherheaded feminine behaviour. And that was what made her fume. Just because *he* was familiar with the East she had to put up with his insufferable superiority!

She was reminded that she hadn't thanked him for coming to her aid at the Al Minbah oasis. But then why should she? He had more or less admitted that the onus of Kamel's behaviour was on his shoulders. At least, she told herself consolingly, *he* wasn't likely to spirit her away to some desert love-nest.

The problem was what to wear. If she made the best of herself McCord would think she had done it to impress him (heaven forbid!). And if she didn't dress up she might find herself politely shunned by the aristocracy of Bahrain. She decided on impulse to go the whole hog and laid out her pearl-grey pleated chiffon. So far McCord had seen her only in simple sundresses.

But it was a matter of extreme importance, she told herself, working a little unsteadily, to be accepted in a society where there was a chance she might unearth Nevine.

Shutting out the remembered feel of a hard chest against her cheek with its accompanying solid heartbeat, she showered away the dust of a visit to the nearby *souk* and was liberal with a rose skin perfume. And rejecting pictures of a dimly-lit balcony with an all-encompassing masculine presence, she reached for filmy underwear and dressed.

The finished result took her slightly by surprise. The dress brought out the silvery lightness of her eyes and the tiny petal-shaped cap of matching material, showing folds of wheaten hair, revealed the slim contours of her throat.

The outfit was ages old. She had bought it just before her father had taken to his bed, and since then there had been so little occasion for dressing up. Still it had retained its freshness she was gratified to note.

Downstairs in the lobby she defied McCord with her look to make any comment on her appearance. Luckily for him he said nothing, though his glance was laconically appraising.

Almost from the start Celia was conscious of a difference in the drive from the routine ones she had made with Kamel. For one thing McCord's personal mode of transport was considerably more luxurious than a company car, and with its cool air-conditioning, motoring, she suspected, could be pleasant.

But it wasn't just the limousine; the driver too was a whole lot different from her over-amorous Arab-guide. If one forgot the expensively tailored suit, and those compellingly attractive-unattractive features, one would still have to contend with a leashed force in the man. In short McCord had a dynamic aura about him, an authoritative air that no lowly Arab employee could hope to emulate.

Rifaa, she had heard, was where the Ruler's palace was situated. It was in the desert some fifteen miles from Manama, and though they didn't actually touch on the Royal abode McCord told her something about the ruined palaces of earlier generations which were dotted on the sandy wastes stretching away into the far distance below the Rifaa escarpment, like a widely scattered desert encampment.

'Most of the owners' families live in modern villas these days,' he said, cruising along the elevated stretch, 'though some of the older members like to preserve the link with their desert ancestry by camping out in the desert in spring, and keeping hawks and saluki dogs. Many of the old robed diehards make for these abandoned courts to pass the time of day among themselves, accompanied by elderly servants and retainers left over from the days when Negro and Abyssinian slaves were fashionable.'

Celia commented with reluctant interest, 'You talk as though you know something about these gatherings.'

'I've been invited on occasions, yes.' His grin was hardly modest, she noticed, perhaps for her benefit. He just couldn't help letting her know how green she was.

'Naturally!' She put enough loaded interference in her reply to shatter his self-assurance, with no effect. One couldn't help sensing, just by looking at the man, that he was something of a force on the island, and irritated further, she mocked in deflating tones, 'I suppose you've had lunch with the Sheikh more than once?'

'I'll admit we're pretty close due to the desalinisation job I did for him in Bahrain.' McCord's light blue eyes were lit with steely whimsy.

Oh, of all the granite smugness! Celia was driven to swinging her own gaze to the front and cursing her luck at being landed in contact with the one man on the island who must be about the worst possible example of complacent male supremacy!

But her annoyance didn't stop her from making the

smooth rejoinder, 'What I can't understand is how they get along with you, these *nice*, unassuming Bahraini types?'

'They're not afraid to learn. Scientifically and commercially there's a lot they don't know about their own country, and unlike outsiders, they appreciate advice.' His expression was bland, but the hint was broad enough. Well, if he thought she could do with some lessons on the East, he was the last one she would approach as a teacher. Add fuel to his already inflated ego by looking up to him with girlish questions? No, thank you!

She decided that the views were a lot easier on her emotions, and soon she saw how the roadside thorn thickets gave way to avenues of oleander bushes and Mediterranean-styled houses with swimming pools, half hidden in a walled-in and green-growing privacy. But what was not hidden from the eye were the kerbside shade trees and tamarisks and servants and attendants gossiping besides flocks of goats. Elegant horses too were to be seen idling in their open-sided barns or airing magnificent manes beneath the trees, giving the impression of a well-to-do community leisurely engaged in the running of its estates.

It was at one of these secluded villas that McCord eventually pulled in. The interior beyond the high walls was green and jungly. Generous trees and flowering plants lined a smooth winding drive. He parked beside other visiting cars expensively solid in appearance. An Arab attendant in local dress hovered and Celia, a little uncertain, followed McCord to the open doorway. He stopped and laying a hand on her arm indicated another path leading through a tunnel of greenery, 'You go that way. I'll see you later.' As the smiling attendant took charge he added, with something like encouragement in his expression, 'It's okay. You're expected.'

Nervous now and trying hard to hide it, Celia followed her guide through the green archway, past dozens of stables and into a courtyard where the silence and emptiness did nothing for her waning morale. They went on down a cloistered walk, and here her glance was drawn to a heap of slippers outside an open doorway. Inside, from what seemed a vast area came the hum of voices. She looked around and finding herself alone on the cloistered walk gathered that this was where she was 'expected'.

In slippered feet she crossed the threshold. It was like stepping back into the past, into another world. At first the darkness was blinding after the brilliant sunshine. Then she began to make out a long, low-ceilinged area, gaudily decorated and stretching for twenty yards or more. And like flurrying petals over flanking sofas and Persian carpets, the room was filled with women, women, women.

There were the gauzy bundles of the local born, bales of saffron yellow, tulip pink and turquoise topped by thick black hair and the shining eyes of the Gulf women. There were also the sleek forms of ambassadresses, cheerful American oil wives, faded English matrons, and the wrinkled-apple faces of the older relatives of the Sheikhdom family.

It took Celia a while to take all this in, of course, for first, as an arriving guest, she had to file with the others down the centre of the room towards the mauve and gold blur which was all they could see of their hostess at the end. A little nearer and she was able to make out a vivacious face, then she was being received graciously by the wife of Sheikh Jussuf Hamed, the owner of the villa and its estates. 'Mr McCord has told me about you,' Sheikha Jamida said in pleasant tones. 'Your father was very fortunate to love a woman of our race, for when we choose the man who will mould our destiny we seldom allow another to take his place, even after death. I do hope you have some luck in tracing the woman of your father's heart. Feel free to enquire here as you wish.'

The sign was given that the allotted time was up and with a grateful smile Celia moved on. She drifted into the comings and goings in the room, into the shaking of hands and sipping of fruit juice and the non-stop chatter. Everything was being discussed, from the latest jewellery recently flown in from Tiffany's of New York, to the more successful ways of growing dwarf tomatoes and climbing roses. No one paid much attention to introductions, the gossip was general anyway, and Celia found no difficulty in merging with the animated gathering.

What spurred her on mainly was the exciting prospect of stumbling upon some clue as to Nevine's whereabouts. Surely amongst all this bubbling femininity, in a stratum of Bahraini society which could well be Nevine's own, someone would know her, or have heard of her.

Getting into conversation was by no means any problem, especially as she chose to mingle with the dark-eyed local women, the only ones really who could help her. And talking about the past was something these ladies delighted in, for to the more mature types they were always 'the good old days', not the bad ones, when *al Khalifa*, the ruler, had been in his prime.

But they were not all as forthcoming as Celia would have wished. Unlike the unprejudiced smile of Sheikha Jamida, some of the listeners considered the act of discussing a dancing girl far beneath their level socially and abruptly changed the subject. Others who would have liked to be helpful were bound to admit that they knew of no such person.

After some time spent drifting from one flower-like group to another with no signs of success Celia was overcome by bitter disappointment. She was beginning to wonder if Nevine had ever existed. Was she just a figment of her father's imagination? A ghost who would never materialise? No, she was real enough, Celia knew, and she was here somewhere in the State of Bahrain. Why she was so sure of this Celia couldn't explain, but nothing would move her from the conviction. And failing to locate Nevine was proving the biggest frustration of her life.

A censer of fragrant burning sandalwood was borne round to which the women leaned in turn to fumigate their hair and drapes. Another gauzy bundle brought round bottles of Christian Dior perfume for splashing over limp hands, and Celia took advantage of the break to slip away. There was no point now in lingering, and she had a curious desire to know what McCord was doing.

As it turned out he was waiting for her at the side of the green archway entrance, looking as though he had been there a while, if one was to judge by the stub of his cigarette.

'Any luck?' he asked, tossing it away as she appeared.

'None at all,' Celia replied flatly, gratified in a way to know that McCord was also thinking of Nevine.

'You've been gone two hours' he said, looking at his watch. 'I was sure you were going to come out with some nimble-footed Arab matron in tow.'

'Has it been as long as that?' Celia couldn't make out whether he was joking or not. Amazed at how the time had flown, she added, 'I hope you haven't been waiting all that time.'

'Hardly.' His grin was expressive. 'We men have our diversions too, you know.'

'I wonder what *they* are?' she asked darkly, making it known by her look that she was well aware of what the Arabs got up to away from their wives.

On this McCord was his usual noncommittal self. 'It's time we were getting indoors,' he said, taking her arm. 'The dinner party will be well underway by now.'

From the moment of entering the split-level drawing room to which they were directed Celia knew that this was top-drawer Bahrain with a difference. In fact it was hard to believe that the two gatherings were taking place under the same roof; one so steeped in the traditions of the East, the other embracing an extraordinary collection of emancipated types who could have compared favourably with any such turn-out at a London, Paris, or New York dinner-party.

All the women were covered in costly warpaint and wafted the most expensive scents. The men, with the same dark eyes and longish features, which were a Bahraini trait, wore suits with the rich sheen of top tailoring. Celia learned from the introductions that McCord made that they were the sons and friends of the Sheikhdoms' families, important men in government circles and business empires. Some of the wives, she discovered, ran smart boutiques and even did jobs of work at the local hospital or some downtown office.

Many of the sleek European women that she had noticed at the soirée had found their way to the drawing room like herself and now they strolled over the acres of deep pile white carpet on the arms of tall, red-faced husbands.

Celia had grown disillusioned with the business of Nevine. It was McCord who indirectly made references to her search during the casual conversations they indulged in around the room. The results of these exploratory enquiries were always negative. Celia hadn't expected anything else.

The drink flowed freely, another surprise for her in an Islamic society. Glass in hand, she admired the picture window framing a floodlit swimming pool and watched McCord being carried off by a dark-eyed beauty with a lovely smile.

Her admiration of the pool and its garden fairy lights waned in preference to following McCord with her eyes. She knew a sneaking desire to study him from a distance, and doing so her curiosity was aroused. What kind of a man was he? One of integrity, she couldn't deny. But what of his social life here in Bahrain? He wasn't married, obviously—unless one could say he was married to his business—but clearly he enjoyed the company of women. There was his date at the Gulf Hotel for one thing, and the flowery bathroom and bedroom she had used at El Zommorro told her that besides accommodating business associates his house was designed to receive women guests as well. Added to this was the European female contingent in Manama.

During her two weeks exploring with Kamel, Celia had learned a lot concerning the local scene. In most of the Gulf region women were scarce, but not so in Bahrain. There were the several hundred air hostesses who worked for Gulf Air quartered on the island, to say nothing of the secretaries, shop assistants and hotel receptionists who came out from England and elsewhere to work in Bahrain.

In this part of the world wives, sisters and daughters were confined to family life, socially, and an expatriate might have to put up with a male society interested only in business; native Arabs who themselves return each day to the feminine solicitude and affection in their own homes, while he has to be content with the lonely life of hotel rooms, or bored evenings in bars. But Bahrain was different. Here there was one thing a European was not, and that was lonely for feminine company. And that included McCord. And the reaction of the svelte, emancipated types in the room to his proximity made it clear that he would have no difficulty on any level.

In what she considered a detached frame of mind on her own part Celia's eyes were drawn to those vital features as he chatted within a group. Surreptitiously her glance toured the sun-brown planes and angles of his face framed by a neat head of dark hair. It was a strong face with hard clean lines; not handsome but oddly commanding. With his big build yet compact frame, he had a charisma she couldn't deny; a kind of effortless charm which put better looking men unexplainably in the shade.

As dinner was announced he drifted back to her side, little knowing that she had paid scant attention to what was being said in her own group. Filing into the dining area on his arm, she was actually conscious of envy among the female members of the party. What a laugh! They didn't know that she and McCord were poison to each other. He couldn't stand her untravelled naïveté and she had had all she could take of his superior male attitude. And that definitely excluded her from his circle of feminine admirers.

CHAPTER FOUR

THERE were three cut-crystal glasses by each place at
the table, and the meal was of such sophistication Celia
doubted whether she would have survived if it hadn't
been for McCord's solid presence next to her. Shyly
mirroring his actions, she got through the successive
dishes, recalling vaguely the bliss of vichyssoise, a cream
soup served chilled, and that the chives were fresh, and
the restrained presentation of the canard à l'orange.

The food may have been European but the conversation was Bahrain, and here again Celia's mood was one
of detachment. All this now was something of an anticlimax to her expectations. She had come here in the
hope of learning something of Nevine, and arriving at
the same dead-end she had encountered in other parts
of the island, she was feeling considerably dispirited.

Whether McCord was aware of this she didn't know,
but fortunately he didn't linger any longer than necessary once the party started breaking up. In the car on
the way back to Manama he asked, 'What are you going
to do now?'

There was no doubt he was thinking of her quest and
she replied, 'What *can* I do? I've explored every avenue
without even the hint of success. I'll have to give up the
idea; forget it and leave Bahrain to its mysteries.'

'Fly back to England, you mean?'

She nodded. 'I was going to go today, but I held off
in the hope that this trip would prove useful. If I'd
known I could have saved myself the extra day on the
hotel bill.' No sooner had the wry comment left her lips
than she wanted to bite it back. She hadn't meant to let
that out.

Outside the desert was a black void below the escarp-

59

ment. Inside McCord was looking like McCord, hard-jawed, supercilious and meditative. 'I thought you were keen to see this thing through,' he said.

'I am! I am!' She swung on him in frustration, then turned to the front again. How could she explain that she was willing to spend a year searching for Nevine but that she just wasn't in a position to do so. How could she say that all the money her father had ever earned had gone during his ill-health? She had spent her own time nursing him, but what did one do in a country cottage where help was not readily available and funds to pay for it even harder to come by? She felt bound to add frustratedly, 'When I first came out here two weeks seemed ample time to do what I had to do.'

How much McCord guessed of her financial predicament she didn't know, but he said no more on the subject. In the silence Celia began to make plans in her mind for a hasty withdrawal from the island. It was late now, but if she packed her things as soon as she got back to the hotel she could leave first thing in the morning and so save herself further expense. Any waiting around could be done at the airport where she could survive on a packet of sandwiches or something until her flight was called.

As she watched the lights of Manama appear that strange melancholy gripped her. It wasn't just knowing that Nevine was here, undiscovered. There was something else that made her regretful at leaving Bahrain. It was odd, this attraction of the East. It wasn't as though there was anything here that was particularly beautiful by scenic standards. She had seen the bleak stretches of the desert, and the island's barren coastline, and the town with its traditional Arab houses and big teak doors was secretive—at least in the old residential quarters—and uncompromising. Yet all of it held some peculiar enchantment for her. It was as though her mind discarded the mundane and heightened the unusual, so that she thought only of shimmering seas and white sand

inducing colour changes around the coast; palest blues
and deep emerald greens, which were dazzling in intensity. Set amid pearly distances the island too was shim-
meringly pale under the desert sun. Topped by a taffeta
blue sky its skyline of buildings, date palms and mosques
rising insubstantially out of the haze had mysterious
charm, a mirage-like quality that evoked an odd response in her.

Realising that she had been dreaming, Celia came to,
to discover that they were now in the heart of the town.
She was familiar enough now with the high-rise blocks
and streets of mud houses that was Manama, yet she
was sure this was not the way to the Gulf Hotel.
Spotting the name of a street that she had no recollection of noting before, she said, sitting up rigidly in her
seat, 'You're going the wrong way.'

'Relax,' McCord threw her a hard smile, 'I'm not
going to carry you off to some Eastern den of iniquity.
I'm just making a slight detour.'

For what? There was no excess of traffic as far as
Celia could see; in fact at this hour of the night the
town was practically deserted. They came to a stop at
last in what looked like a modern building complex. As
McCord came round to open her door for her she asked
coyly, 'Is this part of the detour too?'

'Come and see,' he said drily. 'It's possible you may
consider it was worth it.'

She hadn't the faintest idea what he was talking
about, but as she was relying on him to get her back to
the Gulf Hotel, she didn't see that she had much choice
but to tag along with him.

In the darkness she could just make out the long
black bulk of the building they were making for. At the
door McCord chose a key from the key-ring he carried
and led the way inside. There was enough subdued
lighting to make out a carpeted foyer-like interior and
from here he made for another door. Celia didn't know
what she expected, but it wasn't the sweet, cool draught

of air that hit her on stepping through, nor the fantastic expanse of space that stretched before her. The floor of ice glinted faintly under the sparse lighting and had that eerie quality that all public places of entertainment seemed to possess when deserted.

Because she was puzzled at McCord's choice of surroundings she quipped, 'I've always wanted to see an ice-rink at the midnight hour!'

He moved towards a glassed-in office close by and she followed more out of nervousness at the vast quiet rather than from any particular curiosity. But once inside the spacious interior smelling of new leather and paintwork, which the burst of modern lighting showed as being quite futuristic in design, her attention was drawn to a large photograph over the desk, the only adornment in the office.

The girl in the portrait was enough to claim anyone's glance if the colouring was not overdone, and Celia didn't think it was. She stared at a tumbling mane of chestnut hair with copper lights, laughing russet-gold eyes and a wide white smile that dimpled peach-blushed cheeks attractively. But that wasn't the half of it. It was a full-length photo and below those phenomenally lovely features was a curvaceous form clothed prettily in a short-short skating skirt that displayed to the full a pair of extremely shapely legs. White skating boots and a theatrical stance made the picture a work of art.

'Who is she?' Celia asked, wondering why it irked her to see the photograph so displayed.

'Mandy Bennet, the daughter of an American oil man here, a friend of mine,' McCord said. 'I've known her since she was a tot.'

'She looks like a star performer now.' Celia tried not to sound grudging in her comments.

'Mandy's one of the tops in the ice world.' The grin that accompanied this remark froze any more magnanimous gestures that Celia might have felt obliged to make, and she moved away with a show of studying the rest of the room.

She had no idea that McCord was planning to prolong the social evening until she turned and saw him opening up a cocktail cabinet. 'Like a drink?' he said, setting out glasses and bottle on the desk.

'Are we celebrating something?' Celia asked a little mockingly.

'That depends on you.' That tight smile in evidence, he poured and handed her a glass. She didn't know what to make of being squarely confronted by those somewhat disturbing blue eyes, so she sipped almost obediently and left the way clear for him to go on, which he did with little hesitation. 'I seem to recall you telling me that you'd attained silver medal status in ice-skating. I need someone with instructor's ability to organise the would-be champions who are falling over themselves to learn to skate here.—In other words, I'm offering you a job.'

Celia blinked. 'But I was only sixteen when I passed my silver. I haven't given ice-skating a thought since.' She didn't say that the high cost of training had made further aspirations impossible and that her enthusiasm had soon waned in favour of less expensive pursuits. 'I can't remember the last time I was in an ice-rink,' she finished falteringly.

'Well, you're in one now and I'd like to bet it's like swimming—once you've learned you never forget,' McCord said, sampling his drink. He eyed the huge expanse of ice through the glass partition. 'At the moment it's a bit of a free-for-all here with the blind leading the blind, you might say. An accomplished skater would set the trend, give the young hopefuls an idea of how it's done.'

'Me work here as an ice instructress?' Slowly Celia came round to thinking about it.

'You should cope okay,' the hard blue eyes glinted with something approaching humour. 'At the moment there's only a couple of dozen Arabs who've found the nerve to sample the least known pastime of our degraded Western society.'

'What about the language problem?' she asked.

'You haven't encountered much trouble in that direction so far, have you?'

'No.' Celia had to admit that the Bahrainis, together with the Pakistanis, Iranians and other members of the polyglot race on the island, all seemed to have learned from the same English grammar books.

'It could be the answer to your dilemma,' said McCord with a businesslike smile. 'You can stay on at the hotel, cost of a suite there and meals will be in addition to your salary. And the hours are not long, a couple in the morning and the same in the afternoon and evening. With work you would have a valid reason for staying on in Bahrain, and this would make it possible for you to go on with your search for your father's old flame.'

Celia's grey eyes flared. 'Nevine was not his old flame!' she retorted caustically. 'She was the love of his life, but I wouldn't expect you to understand that.'

McCord propped himself against the desk and relaxing asked, 'What makes you think I don't know anything about this love business you're always toting around like some emblem of a select fraternity?'

Celia thought about it for a moment, then pointed out accusingly, 'You're not married.'

'I'll admit that most men of my age have fallen for some woman's guile,' he shrugged with a cryptic gleam, 'but it doesn't take, necessarily, the marriage vows to make a man a lover. What else?'

She eyed the plush chrome and glass office and the huge expanse of ice outside and replied, 'You're insufferably successful.'

'Meaning that I've never wanted to divide my time between my work and a member of the fairer sex.' His smile was without self-reproach. 'True in a sense, but even a tycoon is not foolproof against the diversions of women as a whole, and surely that's love of a kind?'

'To you men, maybe.' Celia spoke with disdain. 'But that's nowhere enough, nor the basis of true love to a woman's mind.'

'You talk like an authority on the subject!'

At this mocking observation Celia was all at once unsure of herself. True, what did she know of love personally? And was that what McCord was hinting at with his indirect approach? 'My father is my authority,' she said briskly. 'He loved one woman deeply, that I do know, for the greater part of his adult life, and to the end, without the satisfaction of physical contact or reciprocation of any kind. That was some feat in affection, don't you agree?'

'Should be an example to us all,' McCord said piously. Watching her eyes flash their response to his comment, he lowered his glass and straightened. 'But we're digressing; getting away from the subject of this job I'm offering. What do you say? Are you game to give it a try?'

Celia became thoughtful. Something had struck her from the moment that McCord had first made the offer and she voiced her ponderings now. 'You've spent a lot of time and money on this venture, and businessman that you are, I can't imagine that you've done it all without having something lined up beforehand in the way of teaching staff for the place.'

'Well—er——' If it had been anyone else Celia would have said that the lack of firm response stemmed from embarrassment, but with McCord it was simply a matter of finding the right words, of course. 'As a matter of fact, Mandy,' he nodded at the photo, 'was due to fly in a fortnight ago, the day I first spotted you at the Gulf Hotel. I've been waiting for her arrival there every day since, but it looks as though she's not going to make it.'

So *that* was the reason for his frequent visits to the Gulf Hotel! That, or rather she, Mandy Bennet, was his mysterious date, the one that never materialised.

With an odd stab of satisfaction Celia surveyed him quizically. 'Don't tell me the great McCord has been stood up?'

There was something indestructible in his grin. 'Mandy's been doing exhibitions around the Middle East. The last I heard of her she was in Cairo. We had it all arranged for her to take up a teaching post here at the rink's opening, but I guess she must be knocking 'em cold somewhere.'

Celia digested this in silence. She felt a little aggrieved to discover that McCord was simply depending on her to help him out in an emergency. It would have been nice to think that he had suggested the job as a means of helping her in some way, but he was a businessman, she should know that, and in his way he was offering her a deal: a little of her time for the chance to go on with her search for Nevine. It was not a bad bargain, she couldn't explain why she should feel so sour about it.

On the other hand it was tempting to think that she needn't leave Bahrain just yet. She had felt miserable at the thought of having to return to England with nothing to show for her trouble, and one of the things she would miss most, she had to admit wryly, were these abrasive differences of opinion with McCord; even though they always left her emotionally drained.

As she hadn't rushed to give him an answer he probed, 'Got things in England that would make it difficult for you to stay on?'

'Such as what?' Her gaze was questioning.

He shrugged. 'I thought you were carrying the banner maybe, for some young fellow over there?'

Celia coloured slightly beneath the smooth grey petals of her hat. That was the second time in the space of a few minutes that he had made an indirect reference to the romantic state of her own heart.

Naturally she had had boy-friends in the past, but

after nursing her father for two years she had lost touch with that side of her life. However, she didn't see why McCord should know this, so she said, 'There's no one who would miss me to the extent of coming out here to see what's happened to me, if that's what you mean.'

His expression was enigmatic. Because Celia knew he was waiting for an answer she went back to considering his offer. Not that she was in much doubt now regarding her reply. Bahrain had come to mean a great deal to her. And of course the overwhelming plus point was that she could go on looking for the Arab dancer who had long ago won her father's heart.

Because she badly wanted to stay she said, 'If you can supply me with a pair of skating boots and I find I've forgotten nothing of what I've learned on the ice, I'll take the job.'

'Good.' McCord was obviously relieved. He went to a showcase in the office and pointed to a display of top quality skating boots with blades. 'You can take your choice from these in the morning. I'll leave you the key. You should find your size okay.'

They did actually drink on it then and Celia swallowed with a little glow at not having to catch that plane after all. But looking at it another way she did feel that she ought to have her head examined for agreeing to such an arrangement.

All along she had complained to herself about McCord's high-handedness and penchant for running her affairs. Now he *was* her boss!

At the stated hour the next morning Celia drove on the route she had memorised to the Alhambra ice rink. Though it was only a few blocks away the company car, which had been left conveniently parked for her outside the Gulf Hotel, proved useful, for even at this time of the morning the heat was colossal and the air-conditioned interior made it possible for her to arrive as fresh as when she had started out.

She parked the car and went indoors nodding to the cashier in the foyer, and to the Arab assistant in charge of skate hire in the rink itself. After depositing her at the hotel last night and handing over the keys to the office McCord had said that he would be here at the first skating session to help her settle in. But he was nowhere around. The result of having too many business projects to attend to, Celia guessed cynically.

She let herself into the office and chose a pair of skating boots from the showcase. None of the staff interfered with her, so she was obviously expected. She found that her size differed only fractionally from the old days and the soft white kid gave support to her ankles without restricting their flexibility. Once the laces were fastened firmly but not too tightly up her shins she was able to balance around over the office carpet to get the feel of her new footwear.

It was funny how just strutting like this brought back to her all the fun of her teenage days. The smooth surface of ice beyond the office doorway looked inviting, and the eagerness mounted in her to test her abilities after so long away from the sport.

She had donned a pair of stretch slacks in leaf-green and a paler cotton-knit top for her job as instructress, knowing that the consistent cool of the ice-rink would allow her to wear the garments with complete comfort. They proved ideal for her work-out too, for once her blades touched the ice it was as though seven years dropped away from her and she glided and spun, rose in the air and landed with the grace and confidence of her youth.

Of course she knew that her butterfly jumps and arabesque spins were less than perfect and that she would never make a star, but she could skate, there was no doubt about that. And what she knew she could pass on to others.

Lost in the task of testing her skills anew on the ice, she had no idea she had caused a minor sensation until struggling tots on rubbery legs and older children wobbling recklessly like miniature Charlie Chaplins came over to gape. Parents too, keen for the prestige of possessing offspring who had mastered the art of staying upright in this weirdest of sports, crowded at the rail, and Celia was inundated with requests to be shown how it was done.

They had obviously seen nothing like it since the rink's opening, though her own performance, Celia knew, fell far short of what could be achieved with real talent on the ice. Still, she was pleased to know that she had retained much of her confidence and finesse, for what it was worth.

Not being in a position to make comparisons the audience considered her some ice goddess, judging by their admiration. Above the clamour and demands to be shown instantly the secret of her winged feet, she had to make it known that anyone requiring lessons would have to book them in the proper way with the tuition clerk. When it was discovered that one had to pay extra for this service the group dwindled considerably, Celia noted with some amusement, but it still left a sizeable band willing to suffer this added indignity, which would give her plenty to do over the coming weeks.

She felt exhilarated and thirsty after her work-out and decided to make for the bar where soft drinks were sold. Walking on blades took a little more concentration than just strolling in shoes, so that it wasn't until she arrived at the colourfully lit alcove that she spotted a familiar figure viewing the rink from the interior.

For a moment her cheeks grew hot when she realised McCord must have witnessed all that had taken place on the ice. The true test of star material, she reminded herself yet again wryly, was to be blissfully indifferent no matter who was watching. She *had* been utterly carefree. It annoyed her to think it was only this man who would have made her feel stiff and inhibited had she known he was nearby. All the more reason to feel relieved, in a way, that she had not been aware of his presence.

'That was quite a performance.' He supported her by the elbow until she had found a comfortable place to prop against the bar and ordered her a drink.

Celia gave a little curtsy and asked preeningly, 'Do I get the job?' She had no idea what prompted her to behave coyly towards McCord. They had already come to an agreement concerning her employment. Perhaps it was her added stature in skate-boots which helped her to confront his own height and breadth. Or the certain feminine knowledge that her face was glowing and her eyes shining after limbering up on the ice, and to offset the shock of discovering that he could make her feel unsure of herself when performing she wanted to flaunt the confidence of knowing she was looking her best, if nothing else.

McCord said with a grin which was not altogether businesslike, 'I guess you qualify.'

'But not in the same way Mandy Bennet would, I bet?' There she was again, saying things she didn't really want to say; giving rein to this inexplicable impulse to confront him archly when she would far rather not blurt her thoughts aloud.

'Mandy's a world name. She collected medals and cups galore before turning pro.' McCord's shrug was eloquent, though whether this made her something special to him by professional standards or in a more personal way there was no way of knowing.

Celia had sensed his disappointment last night when he had told her that Mandy hadn't turned up for the job. And it was odd how her own small moment of glory on the ice was dampened now by his air of regret. It made her comment a little waspishly, 'It's too bad she left you high and dry with a disorganised rink on your hands.'

McCord's gleam was philosophical. 'There's a saying in the East, *Inshallah*—God willing. Well, in this case Allah appears to be only half willing, but as he's supplied a makeshift answer to the problem I reckon we'll cope.'

And she was the makeshift! While Celia bristled he knocked back his fruit juice and acquiring the look of the tycoon again he added some scant words of praise before preparing to leave. 'From what I've seen of you, you'll make out okay. And by the way, the staff have been informed that they'll be taking their orders from you. They'll be pulling for you whatever policies you decide on for the good of the rink.'

'Hey, wait a minute!' Grey eyes wide, she stopped him as he was about to move off. 'I thought you said that my job was to teach them how to skate?'

'That's right.'

'But now you're talking as though you expect me to run everything around here!'

'Hiring staff for a leisure pursuit that not many people know about in this part of the world was not the easiest of tasks,' McCord explained amenably. 'The ones I managed to recruit are simple souls, they'll need guidance.'

'But I didn't agree to take on the job of supervising your pet venture,' Celia said indignantly.

'Nothing to it. The business runs itself—has been doing for the past three weeks.' Having somehow managed to convey the impression that it would be no comfortable niche despite his optimistic assurances, he eyed her with challenging derision. 'Scared? Afraid that you might make more blunders than you have done already in your two weeks in Bahrain?'

Her dander up, Celia was stung to reply sweetly, 'Have I made all the blunders? You're the one who suggested Kamel as a guide and companion, I seem to recall. And who was it who said I was bound to have language difficulties in my crazy—to you—search for Nevine? But I notice all such obstacles are glossed over when the subject of discussion is the running of your ice rink.' Casting a glance at the olive-skinned clientele who had recently clustered about her in a mildly frightening way, and were now crowding around the booking office for lessons or falling about on the ice, she said, 'I suppose you're aware that I was accosted by all kinds of gibberish out there just now, and wouldn't have known what on earth was going on if I hadn't managed to recognise one or two of the accents as resembling my own.'

'You'll cope,' was McCord's bland reply. Typical, she thought, of a hard-headed businessman interested solely in suiting his own ends.

Nevertheless his challenging speculation annoyed her sufficiently to take on an onus that instinct told her meant trouble by replying, 'Don't blame me if the takings plummet while I'm in charge.'

'I don't think they will.' His blue gaze toured the length of her in leisurely fashion. 'You might prove an asset to the place. In a couple of weeks, who knows, you could be . . .'

'Knocking 'em cold?' she finished for him innocently.

His expression was one of steely appreciation at her wit. 'Something like that.' He gave her a salute before departing.

But once he was out of sight the honeyed smile left Celia's lips and she clapped her glass on the bar with cynical resentment. What a nerve! She'd like to bet that Mandy Bennet wouldn't have had to take on all these extra chores. *She* wouldn't have been expected to practically manage the place while the boss was otherwise engaged.

Then pushing these thoughts to the back of her mind, Celia braced herself for work. What did it matter to her if McCord was sweet on the girl whose photograph hung in his office?

CHAPTER FIVE

HERDING beginners round the ice and offering helpful suggestions to the staff was a lot different from the carefree days of her youth when she had simply skated for the joy of it. But miraculously Celia found that she *was* coping and that so far the Alhambra ice rink hadn't caved in because of her inexpert handling. McCord had said the business practically ran itself—and that figured, she considered now with a curled smile, for he would hardly have trusted her with a venture that would die without his own brain on the job.

After a week she was beginning to know what to expect in the way of patrons at the rink. The morning sessions consisted mainly of children, and these were always accompanied by some servant of the household. They were usually the offspring of the well-to-do of the town, for the urchins had neither the money or the inclination to indulge in the pastimes of the rich. The children, dark-eyed and with the glossy blue-black hair of the Arab, were always beautifully dressed; the girls in panty-short skating dresses, their dark-skinned spindly legs making them look like young fawns on the ice. The boys invariably wore white, the favourite mode of dress being tailored monkey-jackets and slim-fitting slacks. They all took their skating seriously and were acquiring a touch of European sophistication, though their *ayahs* were usually shrouded figures seated at the rail and some of those keeping a sharp eye on the whereabouts of their young charges still wore the veil.

The afternoon sessions were quiet, the heat of the afternoon outside prostrating all but the hardy who made the effort to visit the ice palace mainly for a lark, and to keep cool, of course. It was in the evening when

things at the Alhambra went mostly with a swing. Not
only used for skating, it became a meeting place for
some of the European element of the town and the
coffee lounge, bar and upstairs restaurant were in danger
of becoming quite lively.

Then there were those who were keen to master the
art of balancing on blades. It was strange to see a young
Arab girl in subdued dress clinging to the rail and occasionally managing to glide a few steps, or a thick-set
businessman with his rounded wife in tow laughingly
going on in the local tongue, each giving advice to the
other in the hope of staying upright.

McCord had said that the Bahrainis were proving a
little reticent in braving the unknown of an ice-rink, and
fortunately, with their tightly-knit family customs and
reluctance to shake off old ways, these numbers were
not likely to swell much while Celia was in charge. In
fact while the Alhambra remained just so pleasantly
populated she didn't see that she had much to complain
about—except of course the irritating little hang-ups
that occurred occasionally. Or perhaps she ought to
regard them as the amusing little irritations of an ice-
rink situated in the East.

Like the music incident.

She was painstakingly organising the glimmerings of
a dance session one morning when the wailing over the
loudspeakers made her throw a despairing glance to the
roof. Drums, cymbals, flutes, zithers, all combined to
make a stirring cacaphony of sound; great if you were
watching some desert festival, but no good at all for
gliding around on the ice to.

'One moment, Ahmad.' She left the side of a tallish
eleven-year-old who was showing promise as a dancing
partner and skated off to the music console on the rink's
perimeter. 'Would you mind toning that down!' she
shouted above the din in the booth doorway.

The tape attendant gave her an injured look but did
as he was asked. 'Look, Yousuf,' Celia explained

patiently, when she could hear herself speak. 'You've got to remember that the music you play has to have some bearing on what I'm trying to do out there.'

'But this is the orchestra of the Mahraba desert patrol,' Yousuf's black eyes glowed with nationalistic pride.

'Fine,' Celia smiled lopsidedly. 'But it's not quite the thing for dancing to. What we need is something a little more lilting . . . something perhaps with a waltz beat. I'm sure your stock of tapes include this kind of thing.'

'Waltzes are insipid.' Yousuf's chin jutted. 'We do not understand the West's preference for this type of noise.'

'But you like our popular music, and this often has a very danceable rhythm,' Celia compromised. 'I'll tell you what. If you can remember to play something of this nature for these partnered sessions, I'm sure it will be all right to put on some local Arab pop music for the rest of the time. How's that?' And hurriedly, remembering his national pride, 'And if you like you can open and close each session with something by the Mahraba orchestra.'

Yousuf's face broke into a smile that showed every one of his numerous white teeth. 'I think that is a splendid idea,' he said happily.

Celia recognised that it was only partial victory, but Arab pop music was better than the wail and boom of drums of the desert patrol! . . . Then there was her open conflict with old Ibrahim in charge of skate hire. She still recalled the horror of entering the rink one day and finding a great pile of male and female boots in the middle of the skate room floor. Pairing them up and re-checking the sizes was a monumental task, but no greater than trying to explain to Ibrahim that it just wasn't practical to run a skate hire service on these lines. It was fully three days before she could get him to understand that the pigeonholes around the walls were not there for decoration. But she doubted if they would ever agree on the issue of the patrons' shoes, even though she laboriously explained that rooting through a heap for one's property, as though at a jumble sale, was not done in the best of skating circles.

It was during the second week that she began to feel aware of a certain group who appeared regularly for the evening session. Arabs of high breeding unmistakably, they sometimes wore the cotton robes and headdress but doffed these to reveal expensively cut suits when taking experimental steps on the ice. They were young enough to josh one another while precariously balanced, but were stamped with the successful, and sometimes careworn air, of the businessman.

Their number would vary with each session depending, it seemed, on the whim of the individual, but there was one consistent member of the group whose presence Celia was more than a little conscious of; perhaps because his deep brown gaze always seemed to be following her whatever she did.

The evenings were merry with Yousuf's pop music and the club-like air about the place, but there was always someone who, eager to know the rudiments of skating, booked her time. It was usually while she was stressing the importance of good posture to her pupil and demonstrating the correct way to put one's weight on one's blades, that she would look up and find those brown eyes viewing her with a kind of quizzical interest.

She noticed that this slender-built Arab did quite well on the ice and even when he was unsteady he retained a certain dignity. Because he and his companions appeared to frequent the rink mostly for the fun of it, showing little tendency to take the thing seriously, she was surprised one evening to find that, after she had given some last-minute advice to a pupil, the next one waiting to follow her instructions was none other than the owner of the eloquent brown gaze.

They were gentle and kindly eyes, she noticed at close quarters, though as a teacher she gave no hint of her inner reactions. 'Now the first thing you'll want to practise,' she spoke in friendly but impersonal tones, 'is your edges. There are four edges on each foot, forward outside to left and right, and backward outside to left and right. Now if you'll watch me skate this figure eight, Mr . . . er . . .'

'Rahma,' he supplied, with humour in his voice.

'Right then, Mr Rahma, if you'll observe how my feet are now at right angles and how I push off with the whole of the blade, arms outstretched . . . now see how I lean slightly to the right while keeping my body straight. This gives me a clean outside curve . . . and here is the figure eight done on the outside and the inside of both blades.'

She had a feeling he was watching her perform while paying little attention to what she was saying. But when she asked him to demonstrate what he had learned he tackled the step-by-step routine carelessly but with the untimid grace of a born skater.

Not that he showed much interest in his capacity to catch on quickly. Celia had the distinct sensation that if she had asked him to stand on his head he would have done so, so little attention did he appear to be paying to her coaching.

'You're doing well, Mr Rahma . . . you're very good.' She felt obliged to give him encouragement, especially as she was only stating the truth. 'If you'll take my hand we'll do an inside edge together—it's important, you see, to put the pressure just about here on the blade . . .' She went on giving him tips, knowing that the feel of her hand in his was causing him some bemusement. Well, this was more than evident in his eyes, though she remained aloof from what might have been deciphered as the invitation there. Another Kamel she couldn't cope with!

Mr Rahma reminded her a lot of McCord's office help-cum-guide. He had the same neat build, the same olive-skinned handsome good looks, though these were toned down by a seriousness, despite the smile in his eyes, that Kamel had never possessed. And he was more mature for his twenty-eight or so years too, with an unconscious charm, an air of breeding that singled him out from the others of his kind.

They went on practising for the duration of his half hour lesson, at the end of which Celia released her hand from his and told him, 'You're a very apt pupil, Mr Rahma. I do hope the points I've made will help you to enjoy your skating.'

He stood aside correctly to allow her to move off to other duties, though his look was slightly teasing as he commented in that voice as dark brown as his eyes, 'I can't wait to learn more.'

He was nice, very nice, but Celia, moving off, didn't intend to let her thoughts show. An instructress had to remain impartial, and after her experience with one other young Bahraini she was determined to carry this rule out to the last letter.

She was friendly yet distant whenever she and Mr Rahma met on the ice, but unfortunately this control did not extend to other eventualities, namely the snags that hit the rink from time to time, owing to her precarious management. Like the evening that the ticket machine in the box office seized up.

She had been limbering up on the ice for the first half hour of the session when news came to her that the cluster of people waiting to pay their entrance fee at the door was growing owing to the cashier's mild hysteria at the breakdown of her ticket computer.

Celia had no time to doff her skates, so she clunked out as she was. She hadn't a clue what to do about the gleaming piece of equipment which absolutely refused to produce its numbered receipt or the correct amount of change. And the worst of it was, though the Alhambra was never inundated with customers, they did all tend to converge at the same time, which was what they were doing now, causing an alarming congestion in the street.

Panic taking hold of her, she was unable to think straight. Who among the somewhat unqualified staff could she call on to unravel this muddle? While she was looking about wildly Mr Rahma came through the door into the foyer, also on blades as though he had noted her rapid departure and followed to investigate. She rather suspected this was the case, but was not in the mood to care when he quickly took charge of the situation.

'Pull yourself together, Safia,' he said in his beautiful English to the plump, distraught female figure at the computer machine. And with stern humour, 'This is not an invasion of the Shashriri tribe who carry off women. It is simply a group of people impatient at your incompetence. Here, give me a coin ...' He reached into dish of rejected tender and bent to use a French franc as a screwdriver in the appropriate screw slot. With a few quick turns the press-button fasteners of the removable panel gave way to reveal the jammed machinery.

Celia, stooping with him, watched anxiously. His expressive gaze saying most of what he was thinking, he mentioned only, 'I regret I am not an engineer ... but there are ways ...' And with this he tugged out the entire reel of tickets and slapped them in front of the cashier with the order, 'Tear off the tickets as they are required. And you——' he roped in the services of the hovering door attendant, putting him in charge of the coinage in the lower tray of the computer cabinet, 'hand out the change as it is needed.'

In no time the congestion dwindled to no more than half a dozen people, but Celia looked rueful. 'The tickets are coded and shouldn't be taken out of the machine,' she said uneasily.

'That is only as protection against dishonesty, but McCord knows that no Arab would steal what is not rightfully his. I would not worry about it.'

At this familiar reference to her boss it came to Celia

that McCord had mentioned to her at the beginning
that the ice rink was a whim thought up mainly by his
Arab friends, and she guessed now that Mr Rahma and
his companions were part of this set.

Annoyed at what she considered McCord's gross
neglect of his business, she commented acidly, 'Well, it's
his own fault if he doesn't like the arrangement. He's
never around the place to see what's going on.'

'But he was here little more than ten minutes ago.'
The man who had come to her aid seemed mildly
amused. 'I spoke with him myself before he left. And I
and my friends have often taken advantage of his presence of an evening to meet with him in the coffee lounge
or at the bar.'

Celia digested this with set features. So McCord was
dropping in unknown to her when it suited him to see
that the place was still on its feet. Well, that was possible. While the rink itself was brilliantly lit the alcove
bar and lounges enjoyed only intimate lighting of the
cosy ruby-red type, so that out on the ice, which was
where she spent most of her time, she was hardly likely
to notice who was around.

And then there had been the signs of McCord's brief
appearances during the day: a new set of office keys for
instance, freshly cut and waiting for her on the blotter
of the desk. Her weekly pay packet propped up neatly
in the corner of her clothes locker.

While she was prepared to accept now that McCord
was too canny a businessman to leave the entire running
of the rink in her inexperienced hands it disturbed her,
nevertheless, to hear from Mr Rahma that he was not
the phantom boss she had believed him to be.

For no apparent reason her thoughts flew to what
kind of a picture she made on the ice. Luckily a weekly
income had enabled her to visit some of the better class
boutiques in town, and while she couldn't bring herself
to display too much of herself in an Arab country with
men like Mr Rahma and his friends around she had

nevertheless splashed on several pairs of figure-enhancing stretch slacks in exciting materials and some attractive tops. Though why she should think of this when considering McCord's point of view she wasn't sure.

Naturally she was obliged to look her best in a position where, whether she liked it or not, she was often the focus of attention, but there was no reason to suppose that McCord would care one way or the other as long as she was doing her job correctly. Still it gave her a little glow of satisfaction to know that she had always presented a groomed appearance.

As for her work-outs on the ice, her limbering-ups— was he in the habit of watching them too? With a tingling in her veins Celia recalled her usual carefree way of racing around on blades with the laughter of complete freedom on her lips. And, cross with herself for reacting in this fashion simply because McCord might have been a bystander on occasion, she said tartly to the Arab at her side, 'You're more fortunate than I am, Mr Rahma. McCord is one of those bosses who adopts a kind of sink-or-swim attitude when it comes to advising his staff.'

The cashier had reorganised herself with some difficulty in the unprecedented practice of actually tearing off by hand the tickets of entry, and though still flustered she managed to cope with anyone who loomed up at her window.

Celia saw no reason to hang about, although some thanks were due to the man who had come up with a lightning solution to the dilemma. 'I can't tell you how much I appreciate your help, Mr Rahma——'

'Please!' he stopped her, his gaze lit with mischief. 'You cannot go on insisting on formal terms when we have shared the drama of a jammed ticket roll together. I have another name, also handed down to me by my ancestors. To my family and friends I'm known as Tariq. It would give me much pleasure to hear you address me so.'

'All right . . . Tariq,' she agreed reluctantly, recalling to her chagrin how easy it was to succumb to the Arab charm.

He held the door for her as they re-entered the ice rink area and Celia left him at once with a great show of good duties to perform. Not that this would do her any good, she thought, her smile crooked. Tariq had only to book a lesson to get close to her, and it was patently obvious that he had no burning ambitions where skating was concerned.

But it was McCord who was on her mind for most of the evening. To think that he was often close at hand when she was least aware of it! Of course he didn't drop in for the fun of it, she reminded herself sceptically. As a refrigerator engineer he had to divide his time between the Alhambra and all the other freezing projects he owned in Bahrain. But she would like, just once, to come face to face with him to give him a few home truths about what was lacking in his latest innovation.

The opportunity came much sooner than she expected, and under conditions which were to prove, for her at least, a considerable surprise.

As in all Islamic countries Friday was the weekend in Bahrain, Saturdays being given over to prayer and Koran reading similar to the Christian way on Sundays.

Celia liked the leisurely feeling that always hung over the town on Friday. There was a great holiday exodus to the beach when the oversized cars of the oil-men and their families and the racy Datsuns and Toyotas of the oil-rich Bahrainis crowded the twenty-three-mile stretch of road leading to the lushest seaside spot. There was a gay air too at the ice rink with people dropping in to try their hand (or should she say feet!) at this new-fangled sport before moving on to other weekend pursuits.

She rose after leisurely contemplating the blue sky from her window and let the familiar sounds of city life wash over her as she showered and dressed. Not sounds that one was likely to hear in an English town, she mused; the harsh cry of a driver urging on his team of asses, the shrill rise and fall of bargaining voices in the nearby *souk*. Even the Westernised hum of cars was different, with the gay, uninhibited honking of horns at every turn.

The Bahrainis were very proud of their cars, Celia well knew. Some of the interiors she had seen were like little bed-sitters, with brocade curtains at the windows, brilliant cushions on the divan-like seating areas and ornaments and trinkets everywhere. Once when her own car was being serviced she had had to take a taxi. And that was an experience she wouldn't have missed.

The whole of the inside was done out in shocking pink mohair. From the roof it flowed down over the seats under the feet and even up to the dashboard where the instrument dials were barely visible amid hairy pink wisps. And if this wasn't enough furry puppets with rolling eyes danced at the windows.

There was always something new to discover in Manama, yet she loved the foreign feel of it all and was content at having landed a situation where she could savour it to the full.

Her suite at the Gulf Hotel had the kind of quiet elegance that contributed a lot to this brand of un-rivalled contentment. Apple-green walls and white-flowered curtains were cooling and restful, and ivory-tinted furniture on carpeting of a slightly darker leaf green was her idea of harmonious design.

From the balcony of her bedroom she could see the sapphire blue waters of the Gulf and the view of sunlit minarets gave the living room an exotic flavour. The suite was of villa proportions compared to the single room she had originally booked at the Gulf Hotel, to save funds. Even that had been more expensive than she could afford. But coming out to a strange country alone, and especially one situated in the Middle East, she had felt it would be wise to secure board and lodgings in one of the better class hotels.

This was hardly the term for her mode of living at the moment. She dined in the rose-lit restaurant below, winking with expensive crystal-ware, and there were gardens and a swimming pool at her disposal along with the other guests. At first she had been reluctant to partake of anything more than a roof over her head, but when she discovered that McCord had included all such extras at the hotel in part payment for her services at the ice rink, she saw no reason to forgo the pleasures.

This morning she breakfasted where the heat of the Gulf sunshine was dissipated by gay awnings on a garden terrace, then returning to her suite for a last-minute freshen up and to pick up her things, she set out for the rink. Downstairs she had grown accustomed to coming and going with the air of the working girl, and the grand marble lobby with its numerous businessmen and professionals no longer held any awe for her as it had done in her first days.

She noted that McCord was no longer to be seen around the place. Well, he wouldn't be, would he? Not when his star performer had let him down. Celia wondered if he was finding consolation for Mandy Bennet's non-arrival in the company of the sleek women who graced the parties he went to. Then shaking herself for letting her thoughts drift in this fashion she went out to her car.

The Alhambra, when she arrived, was pleasantly populated but not overwhelmingly so. Her lesson book was fairly full and she got straight down to the business of tuition. The younger children, their *ayahs* in attendance, were showing tremendous improvement, and in their pretty outfits like drifting petals on the ice, Yousuf, for once, playing some imaginative music, Celia began too get the feeling that it was all worth it.

She might have known this serene state of affairs wouldn't last.

By mid-morning she had the horrible sensation that something was not quite right about the ice. It was developing a snowy look across its surface and there was the wet sound of blades skimming through slush. When six-year-old Maryam fell for the third time doing simple edge practice Celia picked her up, brushed her down and delivering her to her *ayah* to dry off decided it was time to go and investigate.

After a speedy change of footwear she hurried round the rink's perimeter with mixed feelings. Melting ice was a serious occurrence, but she wasn't quite sure what to do about it. She followed what she gauged to be the freezing pipes under the rubber floor through a door marked STRICTLY NO ADMITTANCE. In the concrete garage-like space out here stood the Zamboni, a kind of tractor, its function being to shave off used ice on the rink and spray new water which froze immediately.

Nothing ususual in that. What did cause Celia some stunned amazement was the complete absence of any freezing equipment. But that was crazy! She had seen enough of the workings of an ice rink in her teenage years, larking about with friends in forbidden areas and chatting up maintenance men. There *had* to be some kind of machinery—compressors, or whatever they were called—to freeze the ice out there.

She looked around for the local technician, but the place was deserted. The only thing she had to go on was the faint but distinct humming noise coming through open doorways leading into the street. Curiously, her ears tuned, she followed the sound. It seemed to be coming from a huge business concern across the side alley. Bahrainis in working garb were busy trundling cartons of provisions back and forth to waiting lorries. Some in stained white butcher clothing were transferring great sides of beef to parked refrigerator vans.

A big freezing plant. Aha! Now she was getting warmer. Sour humour at her pun changed to a warlike gleam in her eyes as she progressed determinedly, but still very much in the dark, towards an important-looking entrance away from most of the activity.

She climbed a few steps, the hum becoming more pronounced in her ears, and entered a doorway which told her that this was the source of the power she had traced. What she had expected to find she wasn't quite sure, but the scene before her made her grey eyes widen and her jaw drop slightly in awe.

She was in a white moonship-like interior of vast proportions. Gleaming pipes wove intricate patterns around the walls, and complicated dials, switches, winking panels, buttons and knobs made her feel like an apprentice astronaut. But there was nothing out of this world about the set-up, she realised with tightening lips. It fact it was all very down to earth.

Her ice-rink—she didn't stop to wonder at her proprietorial choice of words—was being deprived of vital juice, or whatever it was, so that this ... this ... meat factory could function at full pressure!

Well, she'd see about that! Her curiosity mingling now with a desire for some kind of positive action, she began to scrutinise the white-painted levers ... which one, she wondered, would rejuvenate her melting ice? ... This one with the smart blue stripe round its middle? ... Or would it be this nice red button on a big raised disc? ...

'Don't touch that!'

The voice slicing across what she had thought was a deserted interior startled her to such an extent that her legs almost gave way beneath her. Annoyed at being made to feel caught out, she swung round and lied irritably, 'I wasn't going to,' while her heart reacted peculiarly at the sight of the owner of the voice.

It was McCord, who else! He must have been viewing her from behind glass panels which housed more humming equipment high up in the room.

As he came down the metal stairway his look was not exactly pleasant, being laced with considerable suspicion. 'What are you doing over here?' he asked harshly. 'Your job is to take the customers round the ice, not to wander in places that don't concern you, with a look on your face that says you'd like to put the whole cold storage system out of action.'

These hadn't been quite her intentions, but it was an idea, Celia thought malevolently. This kind of mood coming through in her smile, she said, confronting him, 'It may interest you to know that your precious sides of beef are interfering with my skating arrangements.'

'If you're talking about a slight lowering of pressure,' he studied the sheets of figures on the clipboard in his hand, unimpressed, 'we have an emergency on here. It's been necessary to divert extra energy to cope with it.'

Celia heaved in a breath. She wasn't going to stand there and watch him calmly proceeding with his work. '*Slight* lowering of pressure!' She took him up on the operative word, her grey eyes flaring. 'Maybe you don't know it, but we're on the point of doing our figures over at the rink in ski-snow, not ice!'

'I can't help that.' It was the inflexible McCord talking. 'There are things more important than pretty pirouetting on ice at stake.'

'Well, it's your business,' she shrugged drily. 'If you don't mind running it as a duckpond with toy boats . . .'

'It won't get as bad as that.' He smiled into her battle-warmed gaze, his own insufferably devoid of emotion. 'Technically it's simple. I've had to slow the brine flow, which means the liquid in the pipes under the ice isn't taking the heat away fast enough.'

'Oh, I must say, that's abundantly clear!' Her look said she was more confused.

'Okay, how's this?' in mildly tolerant vein now. 'What we call the freon gas flow—that's what hardens the ice in your rink—has had to be diverted to the factory's own deep-freezes. For the time being this will make your ice slushy.'

'By that I take it you mean for the next half hour or so?'

'Not exactly.' He hedged at her slightly mollified

tones. 'We're dealing with incoming energency shipments at the moment, which means the relay in normal food supplies has been affected. The arrival of local and overseas stock together has created a bottleneck. I need all the pressure I can get to deal with the overload.'

All these lucid explanations! But Celia got enough of the gist of it to exclaim, 'But freezing extra food stocks ... This could go on for days!'

'Or weeks,' McCord acknowledged with the businessman's eye on the main chance.

'But you can't do that to ... to the rink!'

'I certainly wouldn't consider doing it any other way,' phlegmatically he chose to differ, 'for a variety of reasons. The main one being that the Alhambra ice rink is nothing more than a sideline of the real cold storage set-up here. Making use of the surplus of freezing energy normally left over from the plant it was devised, as I think I explained at the beginning, at the whim, and for the novelty and entertainment of friends. I definitely wouldn't put that before the real issue of vast amounts of frozen food stock.'

How could she expect him to? Deflatedly and with some exasperation Celia commented, 'But you seem to take it for granted that I'll be able to hold all the bits together until the situation eases.'

'I'm working on past performance, Miss Darwell.' There was the old challenge in his mocking grin. 'You've taken to the job like a fish to water ...' He ignored her flash of irony, hinting at the fast deterioration of the ice. 'I've seen how you've handled the minor teething troubles of a new business without losing your head.'

'I haven't had much choice, have I?' she retorted sweetly.

'I like to give my key men ... or in your case——' his gleam took in her militant female form without going into details—— 'full rein to run things as they see fit. And by the way, coming back to my personal observations and the visits of those who make up the main patronage at the rink,' was some hint of what made him tick betrayed briefly in his eyes then? 'Tariq's a good friend of mine. I don't want you fluttering your lashes at him like you did Kamel.'

'Oh!' A quivering mass of resentment, Celia swung on him. 'Has anyone ever told you, you are the most aggravating man . . .'

'Why? Because I keep my staff in line?' He had that kind of smile that made her itch to wipe it off with the full force of her hand.

With supreme control she hit back smoothly, 'You don't own me. I'm just a stop-gap, remember? And regarding some of those you employ, you set your Kamel on me like . . . like a friendly puppy. He was all over me within minutes. How do I know that you didn't know full well what you were doing? Perhaps you hoped that one ghastly experience would be enough to put paid to my plans here.'

'Believe it or not,' this sort of theorising seemed to cause him some grim amusement, 'I've got more to do with my time than dream up ways of stopping fool girls who come to Bahrain on harebrained errands. Kamel has had a dressing down for his . . . er . . . over-enthusiasm and won't be doing guide duties for some time. Incidentally,' McCord referred once more to the clipboard in his hand, 'how's the search going for Nevine?'

Celia took a deep breath to reorientate to this sudden change of topic. 'I've chatted with some of the *ayahs* at the rink,' she said heavily, 'and made enquiries whenever I've visited shops in town. You may not realise it, but programming the routines of your learner-skaters three sessions a day is a highly demanding occupation.'

'You want to try organising your time as I do, Miss Darwell.' The male superiority was coming over again. 'I'm having to deal with the emergency here myself, as good ice engineers are difficult to come by in these parts, and I've a dozen and one other projects simmering in town, but I still find time to relax and take a breather in some form or other.'

Succinctly Celia put in, 'I was wondering if you still frequented those parts where Charrière gowns and chunky diamonds are run-of-the-mill stuff?'

Not slow to divine her meaning, he smiled, 'I do sometimes partner one of these dusky ladies.' And then without warning his quizzical blue eyes met her gaze. 'Does the thought bother you?'

Oh, he really was insufferable! All six self-opinionated feet of him! And this in no way included his nauseating male conceit.

'Only in the sense,' Celia aimed at cutting him down down to size before making a serene exit, 'that their ideas on who and what makes pleasant company must be a whole lot different from mine!'

CHAPTER SIX

FROM that day Celia's life at the rink underwent a subtle change. Up to then she had had no reason to know of McCord's cold storage factory across the alley at the rear. But she knew of it now all right—and to her mind it was the cause of everything that went wrong at the Alhambra. The soft ice, for instance. McCord couldn't deny that! The trouble was no one else cared tuppence about the less than perfect conditions. The ice was still delectably skateable for the enthusiasts, and for those who were determined to take it seriously there was the added challenge of trying to fall less often and so keeping the snow off one's clothes.

But Celia, the only what one might term expert about the place, knew that there was room for improvement. She gave lessons as usual and did her bit in other quarters, and no one suspected that anything was any different at the rink. But behind the scenes she conducted a one-woman battle with the rock-like McCord across the street, for better conditions.

If he hadn't enough juice to freeze the Sheikh's joints *plus* her ice, why, she wanted to know, did he build the rink in the first place?

This was an emergency which might not crop up again for another ten years, McCord told her blandly, leaving her to stew in the meantime.

Did he *know* that the ice curtain around the rink, that invisible screen of cold air, was in danger of resembling a south sea breeze and soon, if he wasn't careful, he might have a musically lapping tide to go with it?

'You'll cope,' was all she could get out of McCord as he gave his customary prior concern to his gauges and levers in the moonship-like interior of the compressor room.

Miraculously she did cope, but only, she told herself sourly, because there wasn't one customer here who had any idea how a professionally-run ice-rink operated——Well, perhaps one.

She sometimes suspected that the expressive-featured, quietly vigilant Tariq knew that all was not as it should be underfoot, though even he booked lessons with her and mechanically sailed through the ritual of enlarging his repertoire on ice while making no secret of the fact that it was not her coaching abilities that intrigued him.

She liked Tariq, for although he demanded a considerable amount of her time at these pseudo-teaching sessions he never tried to intrude across the bounds of professionalism. This was not to say that she was entirely ignorant of the fact that he would very much like to if she gave him so much as a hint that she didn't mind.

Each time she recalled McCord's 'fluttering eyelashes' remark she bristled, but there was no denying that Tariq's presence, although he did no more than hold her hand and talk to her with his eyes, was considerably soothing after her abrasive encounters with McCord. Compared to his flinty-eyed charm the aristocratic Arab's warmth and sensitivity was like a healing balm on her emotions.

She supposed that sooner or later they were going to have to get to know one another better. There was a limit to how much of a barrier one could sustain with a man who was in every essence a gentleman. The moment came one evening when she was sipping a much-needed cup of coffee after making sure that all was as it should be in the rink. Tariq, his own cup and saucer in his hand, drifted over and asked, 'May I join you?'

'Of course.' Celia hedged only slightly. The lounge was almost deserted and there were plenty of free tables, but she knew it would have been petty to refuse the Arab's request.

He lowered himself into the seat facing her and stirring his coffee said with his expressive eyes, 'You have
the look of a mother swan whose chicks have been mis-
behaving all day.'

She looked faintly amused and replied drily, 'Thanks
for the compliment, but I don't feel very swan-like
skating on a surface that McCord fondly terms as
ice.'

'He has his problems.' There was nothing more irritating than one man defending another to a woman,
especially the one who is the very source of upset, but in
Tariq's case Celia couldn't take umbrage. The genuine
concern and affection he showed for his friend in no
way detracted from the sympathy he felt for her. 'There
is tremendous pressure on at the moment to house all
the surplus stock of perishables, but everything will be
in order again soon, I am sure.' His very manner was
consoling, and while she knew that he couldn't be
expected to understand the situation as she did she
smiled and changed the subject with, 'What do you
know about swans anyway?'

'I have seen your swans of Abbotsbury,' he twinkled
proudly, 'and those on the lakes in your parks. But it is
wrong to associate them only with cooler countries. We
too have a park some miles out of town—admittedly
only newly developed—and there are a dozen or so of
the species quite happy there. With the right degree of
refrigeration in the water——'

'McCord again!' Knowingly Celia couldn't help
sounding tart.

She sipped her coffee and found Tariq's warm but
searching regard unsettling. She had never before met a
man who could break down the barriers of reserve with
just a look. 'You do not have the mental make-up for
this kind of work,' he said with shrewd humour after
some moments had elapsed. 'Tell me, how is it that you
are working here for McCord?'

That was a very good question. Celia knew that she

had long since grown away from her old affinity with ice. Her enthusiasm for donning skate-boots and speeding over mirrored surfaces had faded with her teenage years, and certainly she could think of more exciting things to do at the moment than instructing mainly frivolous patrons how to remain in a perpendicular position.

True, she wanted to stay on the island in the hope of tracking down Nevine. But work was easy enough to come by in Bahrain, she had discovered some time back. So why was she doing the job? To help McCord out? Did she care whether this lame venture of his survived or not? Another very good question, and one which along with the others she didn't feel disposed to answering at the moment. Though she made a reply in kind to Tariq.

'I came to Bahrain on a sort of mission,' she said, not wanting to bore him with details of her father's past life. 'It . . . well . . . ran into difficulties. McCord's choice for the job, a girl he had in mind to act as central figure at the rink, had let him down, and I needed time to make . . . alternative plans, so I stepped into the breach, you might say.'

'You have exceptional organising talents, but I do not think you are happy playing nursemaid to so many lame dogs,' Tariq joked perceptively.

Happy! That was something else that Celia hadn't given much thought to up to now. She certainly wasn't glowing at the way her life was turning out at the rink, though she couldn't explain why. It had nothing to do with her frustration at present conditions, that much she knew.

She countered Tariq's intuitive probing with a smiling, 'How many of us are completely content in our workaday lives? I bet you come to a dead-end sometimes.'

'International shipping is not the easiest of vocations,' he admitted with a lighthearted sigh. 'But as a member of a family who have been in the line since the days of the old pearling dhows I am committed to do my part.'

Sitting across from him Celia couldn't help noticing his sensitive mouth, the luminous warmth of his dark eyes, and the way the wiry waves of his hair framed attractively his smooth olive-skinned features.

She was bound to make some comment then to fill the somewhat unsettling pause that stretched as his gaze held hers. 'As a shipping magnate,' she said truthfully, 'you don't appear to have an awful lot in common with the down-to-earth pastimes of an ice rink.'

'It has all been one big and rather enjoyable joke,' Tariq laughed, showing teeth reminiscent of those pearls his forefathers used to gather. 'We asked McCord to give us something to work off the stale cramp of sitting at an office desk all day. Exercise we have been taught to respect as the alternative to coronaries and arterial complaints.'

'There is all kind of sport here for the businessman, so I'm told,' Celia shrugged.

'But where in Bahrain,' he had a rather engaging grin, 'is it so cool?'

He had a point there. Celia had to admit that she had hardly noticed the heat since her employment at the rink. She supposed she had McCord to thank for that. Drat the man! Irritably she shut off this avenue of thought. She didn't seem to be able to keep him out of her mind for more than five minutes at a stretch.

She said with inquisitive humour to Tariq, 'I get the feeling that you and your friends know something of the adventures of ice skating?'

'My colleagues and I are not new to the bruises that can be collected in the art which you achieve with ease,' he commented with a goodnatured grimace. 'There is quite a grand ice palace in Kuwait. We have been there several times in the past. The interior is as big as a barracks and there are all kinds of cups to be won for keen competitors. But of course it is more convenient to shed one's weight nearer home.'

Eyeing his lean frame, Celia remarked mischievously, 'You hardly qualify for the title of overweight dyspeptic, Tariq! I suspect you and your chums throw yourselves around for the pure hell of it.'

'But I can be serious when it suits me, as you have seen,' he contested with a teasing light. 'And who knows what heights I might attain as your partner on ice. I'm thinking we should practise our talents elsewhere. Fly with me to Kuwait. I would very much like to show you the ice palace there.'

Here it came! Gentleman he was, with courtesy and breeding, but he was still an Arab. And Celia had to keep reminding herself that they conducted their love-life as they ran their high-powered cars—without a minute to lose!

This was the first real conversation they had had since meeting, yet he calmly wanted to whisk her off to Kuwait as though it was a bus ride to the next village!

'I'm afraid I've no time for travelling, Tariq,' she said lightly, thankful to have a valid reason for refusing. 'Three sessions a day keeps me busy here.'

'But in a week's time we have a public holiday in the Arab calendar.' Tariq thought of everything. 'On that day all places of entertainment will close, so you will not have to work, you see.'

'But if the ice rink's closed here, won't it be the same in Kuwait?' Celia asked innocently.

'Ah!' Perhaps Tariq didn't think of everything. With laughter in his eyes he shrugged, 'Well, Kuwait has some very fine scenery.'

They were both laughing at his audacious tactics when a big-built figure moved into the coffee lounge. McCord had seen them before they had seen him, Celia knew, and for this reason she went on making small talk with Tariq. All but the hardy had left the rink and the few beginners were having a last fling before it closed. They needed no help from her, so Celia purposely remained seated. She wasn't going to jump up guiltily just because McCord had appeared. She might work for him, but she wasn't his slave!

He approached their table with a kind of lazy indifference which somehow didn't match the look in his eyes. 'Don't believe anything she says, Tariq. She tries it on all the Arabs.'

He might have been joking, but Celia caught the mocking undertones and her eyes ground sparks as they came up against his.

'In that case I am delighted to be in the line of fire,' Tariq joked back. 'Won't you join us, my friend?'

Unfortunately McCord slid down into one of the other chairs at the table. The air vibrated with his presence, and striving to ignore the fact Celia kept her attention smilingly but grittingly with Tariq.

'I did not go to the Alirezas gathering myself, but I see you were unable to fix up a similar plea of a "previous engagement",' the Arab deduced with humour.

McCord's casual attitude as he lounged at the table did little to detract from his suave appearance in superbly cut suit and white dress shirt. It was obvious he had been out on the town somewhere, Celia also deduced cynically.

'The party was more than average entertaining, Tariq,' he laid it on, no doubt for her benefit. 'Your people have a lot more tricks up their sleeve than you give them credit for when arranging occasions of this nature.'

'In the shape of lustrous-haired females in expensively simple attire,' Tariq twinkled knowingly. 'I have seen them all, my friend. But for you perhaps it is still an adventure.'

'I don't tire that quickly, Tariq,' McCord's grin was expressive and what was worse, all-encompassing. Celia sat there pretending, with difficulty, complete detachment. 'My staff don't approve—' if he went any further she would locate his shin beneath the table with the nice steel blade of her skate-boot, '—but to my mind there's no better way of relaxing after a hard day's work.'

'You have to understand what he's going through, Tariq.' On the other hand Celia decided perhaps words of a kind were more ladylike. 'He hasn't mentioned it to a soul, I bet, but he's really drowning his sorrows, you know, because his true lady-love failed to turn up as expected.'

'Ah yes, the one who is still floating around in Cairo.' The fact that Tariq knew that much about the absent skating queen caused Celia a dull shock. If she had been discussed between the two men to this extent then Mandy Bennet was a lot more substantial a figure in McCord's life than even Celia had supposed.

'In that case,' Tariq assumed the heavy air of a sympathetic heart physician and slapped his friend's shoulder, 'I recommend a dose of lovely ladies at least once a night.'

This kind of trying conversation, for Celia at least, went on for some time with only Tariq unaware of the subtle innuendoes that gave it bite. McCord's eyes, when they met hers, were lit with lazy malice, but this was nothing, she hoped, to the message of sweet hate that issued privately from her own.

But for all the emotionally draining experience of making apparent light chat with the boss present, closing time came round with her barely noticing it.

The rink had emptied and all the coffee cups had been washed and stacked. It was McCord who rose first, drawing her attention to the fact that the rest of the staff were hovering in the background, anxious to be off. For this reason she idled on at the table finishing a lingering conversation with Tariq about the pearling banks in the Gulf.

At last the Arab rose, after a large hint from McCord with the dipping of the coffee lounge lights. But Tariq was in lingering mood still and as they moved out into the rink area he put an arm round her waist, though she was perfectly steady in her skate-boots, and laughed, 'You see what a fine team we make!'

It was an excuse to revert to a previous conversation, Celia suspected, and sure enough, his smiling dark eyes questioning, he asked, 'What about our date? Will you come with me to Kuwait?'

Celia was breathless. Tariq's nearness was heady enough for any woman. With those dark good looks, his charming personality, and the undeniable attraction of the well-bred Arab, she had difficulty in keeping her boot-clad feet firmly on the ground.

In the shadowy glow of the rink's perimeter she demurred, 'I'll have to think about it, Tariq.'

'If that is what you are going to do, then I am happy.' His quietly elated look told her he had taken her words as an acceptance. He fastened a cotton burnous about him to go out into the street, and flaring as he walked, it gave him the appearance of a dashing desert figure.

Celia watched his departure in the gloom with excitement singing in her veins.

She came to shortly afterwards, aware of McCord's shadowy shape locking up the music console apparatus, not far away. Cooly ignoring him now that there was no longer any need to put on a polite front for the benefit of others, she made straight for her private locker in the office.

She heard him checking distantly on things around the rink, and feeling wryly that the office was hardly big enough to accommodate the two of them plus the antagonism which seemed a little rife between them at the moment, she hoped to make a hasty departure. But luck would have it that the lace of one boot knotted up, perhaps because of her fumbling fingers, and McCord drifted in while she was still scouting for her shoes.

Fortunately all was in order on the desk. There was not enough going on at the Alhambra to involve a lot of work behind the scenes, and what bills had come in for ordered cartons of drinks or fresh supplies for the upstairs restaurant Celia had laid neatly on the desk.

McCord flicked through them casually. In the bright lights of the office, compared to the dimness on the outside, he was a dominating force which wouldn't be ignored, though Celia worked at it.

He said, tossing the bills down again in a way that boded fresh skirmishing, 'How long have you been selling tickets off the roll instead of through the computer?'

So he was in *that* kind of mood, was he?

'As long,' she said with sublime indifference, 'as your mechanics have failed to find the cause of the jamming metal rod that holds them.'

'The cashier has strict instructions to make no sale of tickets without a computerised check,' he said, moving round the side of the desk.

She had her shoes on now and she skirted him with just the right degree of healthy respect to search for her car keys in her handbag. 'Instructions are all right,' she replied tightly, 'if you're around to back them up. But while you're glued to gauges and thermometers back there,' her glance clearly indicated his meat factory across the alley, 'someone around here has to think fast enough to avoid a police caution for obstructing the pavement outside.'

Surprisingly he grinned, but it wasn't a nice sight. 'You're not telling me it was your nimble-witted idea to deal manually with the customers? As I heard it was Tariq who came to your aid originally when the reel got stuck.'

So he knew all about that. And he knew the ticket office was still causing problems. *His* ticket office. But he was calmly trotting out these malfunctions as though the onus was on *her*.

Oh! Her anger became a quivering nerve in her throat. The worst of it was she couldn't find half of the things she needed to leave, and this involved bypassing him

several times to various corners of the room. The sadistic
pleasure he was deriving from playing the dissatisfied
boss was apparent in every muscle of his suavely
groomed frame. And on top of this Mandy Bennet's
likeness smiled down on her from the wall over the desk,
the silent laughter on those lips, the sparkling friendly
eyes lending an almost comical irony to the tense and
crackling atmosphere of the office.

When Celia could find her voice she made it sound
deliberately smooth. 'Tariq has proved a wonderful help
in a lot of ways at the rink. At least the customers don't
mind rallying round, even if the owner is for the most
part . . . otherwise engaged.'

The emphasis she put on the last two words was
unmistakable, but McCord only sloped his unpleasant
smile.

'Perhaps it's the staff who induce the rallying round
impulse,' he said hatefully, hinting no doubt at her long
session with his Arab friend at the coffee lounge table
tonight. 'As I see it Tariq is just a patron and it's not
his place to become involved in matters of policy at the
rink.'

'Who said anything about matters of policy?' Celia
curved her lips into the semblance of a smile, also hinting at her lengthy tête-à-tête with Tariq. The subtle innuendoes in this remark sent her exhilaration soaring. It
felt so good to get one back at McCord, even though
she was making more of her brief relationship with Tariq
to satisfy this burning desire.

But while she put on an air of being in complete control of her feelings Mandy Bennet's merry sparkle following her wherever she went made her want to scream.
It was not the first time she had felt the suffocating
awareness of the photograph in everything she did
around the office, and in the heat of the moment now
she was tempted to fly at McCord with the exasperated
request to remove the offending image of loveliness.

She didn't, of course. Feminine intuition advised

strongly against this kind of hysteria. It was only a photograph, after all, and even if the flesh and blood of it was in McCord's mind most of the time ... well ... an olive-skinned face floated mentally before her vision, one with fervent dark eyes, quizzical invitation in their depths, and she found the thought of Tariq oddly comforting in that moment.

She unearthed her car keys at last in a drawer of the desk. McCord, who had reacted not at all to her subtle comment that she might have other things besides work to discuss with her friends—well, he was a man of steel anyway, Celia mused in disgust—followed her movements with something of a blue glint. Seeing that she was ready to leave didn't stop him from labouring the point over outside interference at the rink.

'Just remember to keep your mind on your job, Miss Darwell,' came the drawling order, with just the right degree of implication that McCord was past master at injecting into his tones. 'Who knows, you might find that the only ones disposed to rallying round you then are the ones who get paid for it.'

Celia dropped her car keys into her handbag and picked up her dressing case. She had had about enough of McCord for one evening. 'Going by conditions of late,' she sailed past him, 'we might all find shortly that your sole clientele at the rink are the ones who get paid it.'

'I doubt it, Miss Darwell,' his voice floated sardonically after her as she barged away along the dimly-lit route towards the street door. 'With you in attendance I doubt it.'

Celia gave him the frigid length of her departing figure as reply. Oh, he could harp on about her friendship with Tariq in his underhand male way, but he needn't think that she was going to hang around to listen. And now when she came to think of it the idea of flying to Kuwait seemed very attractive indeed. She had told Tariq she would consider his invitation and so she had.

At the moment she could think of nothing nicer than joining him on the public holiday he had spoken of, for a flip to another Arab country.

But the day in question was a week away, and with the air charged as it was between her and McCord, she was to discover that a lot could happen in that time.

CHAPTER SEVEN

As a means of shutting out of her mind the trials of the ice rink Celia decided to renew her efforts in the search for Nevine. Though her six-hour working day tended to sap her once glowing enthusiasm in this respect she discovered that her free time, between the afternoon and evening sessions, was ideal for venturing abroad. It was cooler then and the town came alive with the real business of the day being done in the shops and bazaars and gleaming blocks of offices.

Taking the car or sometimes going on foot, she wondered how she could have believed in the early days of her arrival that Bahrain was anything but a true portion of Arabia. Her first impressions of a Westernised air about the place now seemed like an illusion as she explored the rectangular warrens and alleys of Manama, with its tunnels and courts, little lock-up shops, and donkey stalls on streets that were little more than arm's-width passages made narrower by the constant flow of humanity.

Often the only European in sight amid varying skin colours and modes of dress ranging from the black veil to camelhair robes and flowing caftans, she pierced the veneer of Manama's outward sophistication to find a centuries-old culture that no amount of foreign influence could eradicate.

Along one narrow alley the scent of teak and pine spoke of carpenters at work. Another was a brilliant stream of Eastern cottons. The goldsmiths too had an alley to themselves, tapping away with their little hammers and a patience as old as time.

One could shop for meat, vegetables, spices and clothing along lanes where conflicting scents and odours knew no boundaries, and the residue of pungent basil, mint and coriander, fresh sawdust, roast coffee, musky perfumes and the barnyard effluence of live chickens lingered like a pall over the neighbourhood.

Frequently it was a shock for Celia to emerge from the world of mud dwellings and cobbled byways to find herself after all in the twentieth century. Even the marble, glass, and concrete of modern Manama failed to dull her growing awareness to the fact that under these blue skies, pearl-sheened by the heat, was a civilisation steeped in the traditions of the East.

But whether she chose to wander in the native quarter or to drive around the more sophisticated residential areas, she made no progress in her search for Nevine.

She knew very little Arabic and though English could be used on occasion it was difficult to start up a conversation which involved going back thirty years in time. Merchants and business people were concerned only with living the impact of the moment, for it was today's takings that counted, not those of three decades ago.

Accompanying Kamel it had been different. With the Arab arrogance of one who has obtained a slightly exalted position in his job he had barged in on the most intimate of business deals or domestic discussions to put his questions across. But Celia was not in a position to behave in this manner, nor quite frankly did she have the nerve. Also in her weeks in Manama she had made an important and not too promising discovery.

Though foreigners and Arabs may live side by side in Bahrain, one was always conscious of the invisible barrier that separated the two societies. Each lived their own lives according to their own customs, and though friendships may blossom and even deep affections there was this unwritten law that kept the Arabs to themselves.

This was one of Celia's main despairs when she thought about her longing to meet Nevine; and the possible obstacles that might prevent this; especially as she was convinced more than ever that somewhere in these multitudes was the woman of her father's heart, and that it was only ignorance of her whereabouts that separated them.

What with her difficulties at the ice rink and her failure to meet with any kind of success regarding her reason for visiting Bahrain, Celia was not in the chirpiest of spirits these days. But there was one aspect of her work which gave her considerable pleasure, and that was the coaching of her star pupils on ice.

Since the early days when they had resembled wobbly-footed elves on blades, the children of the morning sessions had come a long way. Now they skated with the grace and precision of serious professionals, and there was a good half-dozen who showed the makings of budding champions.

Considering the upheavals that Celia had to contend with she was more than a little proud of the headway she had made with her brood, and seeing the *ayahs* nodding and beaming at their charges from the seats round the edge, she suspected she wasn't the only one to feel this way.

Always prettily dressed, the little girls were lightly moving fairies on ice, the boys like miniature gallants in their wake. It would be an idea, Celia mused at one of these sessions, to harness the talents of the children and put on some kind of show.

But where she would find the time to organise a display of this sort was another question. As Jack—or Jill—of all trades at the rink, she found herself doing jobs that were nothing at all to do with her supposedly exclusive position as ice instructress.

The restaurant, for instance. It had a staff of its own, but who would believe it! In exasperation one morning in the office Celia glowered at the catering release slip in her hand which would have to be signed by McCord. How they managed to lumber her with their responsibilities she was never sure. What she did know from past experience was that if she went upstairs now the restaurant would be mysteriously empty, everybody seemingly busy as usual elsewhere with preparations for opening at sundown.

She left the slip until she was no longer needed on the ice, then changing into shoes went across the alley to the cold storage factory. If she didn't act there would be no food for the restaurant tonight, though why *she* should worry about that . . .? Sourly Celia dismissed the thought and went up the steps into the compressor room.

McCord was in his glass-panelled den high up in the room, and realising after some time that he had no intention of coming down, she was obliged to negotiate the metal stairway into his humming, bleeping domain.

It really was an education to see just what lay behind a little bit of freezing for food storage plus—though why mention it? she thought cynically—her own expanse of ice.

McCord was hardly the scientist in appearance, in well-cut suit, the jacket of which he had tossed over a pipe-junction, his once spruce shirt tugged open at the neck giving disarray to the businesslike knot of his tie.

'You picked a great time for a visit,' he said, rapidly turning a big wheel and watching the reaction closely on a nearby meter face.

Ignoring his sarcasm, Celia asked with an unexplainable desire to get in his way, 'What's that red liquid bobbing up and down?'

'It's the P.S.I. meter,' he explained grimly. 'Pressure per square inch to you. We need another cold room and I'm having to watch the refrigerant fluid.'

With a bored air she waved the chit under his nose and asked, 'Would it survive without your tender care long enough for you to stamp your authority on this?'

He didn't look at the piece of paper in her hand, only at the needle on the gauge to the right of the wheel. When it swung to dead centre at the top of the glass he relaxed his frame slightly and breathed, 'That's better. Now we've got ideal pressure.'

'We?' Her query was delivered mockingly and not a little bitterly. She spared a glance around. 'If I could find the ice rink pressure among all this paraphernalia of levers and switches I'd like to bet it would register anything but "ideal"!'

He ignored that trend of thought, also the catering chit, in favour of another urgent swing of a wheel. Feeling slightly ridiculous left with arm outstretched and the yellow slip fluttering at the end of it like a limp flag, Celia gave up for the time being and drifted round trying to make some sense of all she saw. There was a chattering Telex among a nest of similar machines in one corner. Idly she picked up the jumping tape and read an order being put through for smoked salmon, caviar and a lot more to be delivered to the Sheikh's palace for a forthcoming banquet.

This must have been something McCord was expecting, for he crowded over her to absorb the message himself, rapidly typing back a reply, before swinging back to the all-demanding task of keeping the needles and red liquids happy.

It occurred to Celia, since she had made the remark, that it might not be a bad idea to do some surreptitious scouting for the ice-rink pressure gauge. It would be here somewhere and it *would* be interesting to see what it registered compared to the rest of McCord's pampered equipment.

She must have examined every clock face and meter gauge in the place before she finally spotted it across a space whose distance did nothing to dim the damning evidence before her eyes, of a half-cocked lever.

Well, if that wasn't cheeky! She had no time to take a

closer look—not that she needed to, for McCord was
suddenly by her side. He flicked the slip of paper from
her fingers and signing asked, 'What that be all, Miss
Darwell?'

The challenging whimsy in his blue eyes told her that
he had noted the direction of her gaze. His inflexible
smile also indicated that he had no intention of ac-
nowledging it.

'That's more than enough, *Mr* McCord,' she whipped
the slip from his hand and made a wooden retreat.

Her connections with the Alhambra restaurant had
never been more than shouldering the load of its work-
shy administrators, until one evening when Tariq asked
her to dine with him there. It had been a particularly
exacting day and the thought of lingering in the rose-lit
interior whose windows looked over the ice rink at one
side and the multi-coloured lights of Manama at the
other was attractive indeed. Especially as her companion would be a man she both liked and was strangely
attracted to.

She had had no time to dress for the occasion, but
sitting in a lamplit glow later, a pretty lace top she had
donned for the evening session more in evidence than
her slacks under the table, she didn't feel that she was
too much of a let-down to Tariq's refined appearance.
If she was on view from the office and the shadowy
reaches of the rink, now deserted, so what? she mused
rigidly. Her work was finished for the day. And in her
free time she pleased herself.

The meal was surprisingly good, mellowing her opin-
ions of the restaurant staff. Not that Tariq paid much
attention to what was placed before him. He wanted to
know all about her. They talked. She talked. Inevitably
it came out about Nevine and Celia's frustrated attempts
to find her. She wondered why it hadn't occurred to her
to mention it to Tariq before. With his shipping business
and family connections he knew a considerable cross-
section of Bahraini society.

Disappointingly his response was negative. He'd never heard of such a person, nor could he offer any suggestions on how she could be traced. Of course it was obvious by the look in his eyes, which for the most part rested on her, that he more than anyone she had accosted so far had a burning interest in the present, not the past.

Lightly she let the matter drop and for the rest of the evening she allowed her feelings to run riot a little under his intoxicating gaze.

As she had her own car they parted in the restaurant doorway at a lateish hour, but not before Tariq had raised her hand to his lips and brushed them lingeringly around her wrist and with pressure in the palm of her hand, in a form of farewell.

In a way Celia was glad that she had other things to think about beside this dark-eyed Arab with the charming manners.

She put all her efforts into coaching the children in a form of ice-ballet musical interpretation. They were greatly excited at the idea. Each was allowed to choose his or her musical piece, and as enthusiasm grew the costumes visualised were startling at times. Ahmad insisted on interpreting a James Bond theme and saw himself in tight black trousers and shirt, and a gun in one hand. A water pistol, of course. Did little Arab boys have those annoying toys too? Celia wondered in private amusement.

Iffat and Zaki Junaid had decided to do Romeo and Juliet. They were both sensitive little performers and their practising on the ice to the rather touching music brought an ache to the throat of all but the hardiest among the onlookers.

Celia's work had gone rather well at the rink lately. This alone ought to have warned her that it couldn't last. She was used to nursing several grievances at a time over unprofessional conditions at the Alhambra. It was uncanny indeed not to have one grumble worth voicing; rather like an uneasy calm, she felt, that usually preceded trouble.

Sure enough it came, in the shape of puddles on the ice one morning when she was putting the star performers through their paces. This was to be the complete run-through of the progress they had made so far in the construction of the ice ballet, and the insidious suspicion of water slowly taking the place of the hard polished surface she had always insisted on, together with glistening stretches which were beginning to twinkle weirdly under the roof lighting, made Celia, after all her efforts, see red.

This was the limit! This was more than the last of the last straws!

She told the children to practise limbering-up exercises at the rail until she returned, and after cursing every moment it took her to change into suitable footwear she moved with seething determination towards McCord's cold storage warehouse.

She knew what she was going to do. It ought to have been done a long time ago, and never more than now would she enjoy the counter-blast of exacting what was her due.

There was a white-coated assistant in the compressor room; a bespectacled Bahraini who looked up from the figures and notes in his book at her appearance. Like a whirlwind Celia gusted past him, making straight for the metal stairway. That his jaw had dropped in her lightning passing caused her not an iota of concern. In any case her mind was otherwise engaged reorientating herself to the upstairs laboratory and the whereabouts of the lever that indicated pressure at the ice rink.

She found it with not much stalking around. As usual it was half-cocked. Well, this was something that was going to be changed, and *drastically*, within the next second or two! In half that time she knew the satisfying feel of cold metal in her hand, was poised to push the thing exultantly all the way home, when a hand clamped down on hers and a voice breathless from the dash to reach the lever before she did ground out, 'Get your fool hands off that pressure!'

In the latticework of pipes and fitments she hadn't noticed McCord in the vicinity. But it wouldn't have made any difference if she had. Her determination to see justice done once and for all didn't stop with his appearance; though the steel bands of his preventive embrace were making a good job of squeezing the breath from her lungs.

The pinpoints of fire in her grey eyes emphasised her defiance and all-out intention to upgrade the lever anyway. His own flame-lit look was menacingly and persuasively to the contrary. Celia couldn't think of anything in those seconds that would give her more supreme satisfaction than thwarting his orders.

Clamped against McCord she might have been pitting her strength against the original iron man. Her fingers were growing limp on the lever, and as she fought madly against capitulation the blue eyes blazing into hers were calmly telling her she would capitulate anyway.

Both breathing furiously, neither giving an inch—mentally at least—Celia contended while her body began to cave in. It was a paramount battle of wills, coming to a head as breath mingled with battling breath.

At last Celia threw her head back, her fair hair awry as she gasped for air. Relentlessly the victor, even after her hand had dropped lifelessly from the lever, McCord's steely regard was smoulderingly, and curiously immovable. She felt nailed by the odd light in his eyes, awash in some new emotion that she knew only as a piercing disturbance within her.

So close to the man whom she seemed to have spent her life bickering with, she found she had suddenly run out of steam; though her blazing gaze continued to hit back to cover up her disorganised flow of thought.

Locked together like this, McCord's bone-snapping

grip on her, the moments seemed to stretch into eternity, and strangely suspended Celia had nothing to offer to end the scorching impasse. Then as he abruptly let her go, it was several seconds before McCord erupted afresh, verbally this time on her ignorance of freezing methods.

'Have you any idea what chaos you would have caused if you'd pushed that lever home?' he rounded on her. 'All the cold rooms have an automatic safety level, but because of the size and nature of the ice rink the only safety valves it possesses are here in the compressor room. And *because* there's a mile of pipes under the ice there's what's called a 'flow-delay', which means that we have to wait up to ten minutes at the pressure wheel to see that the P.S.I. doesn't go too high for the rink— *otherwise* the gas would find a weak point in the tubing and blow a hole through the ice—*And* the refrigerant fluid could start leaking as a gas, and let me tell you those fumes are dangerous——'

Considerably sobered by the technical implications of his explanation, Celia was nevertheless aware that he kept his *own* cold storage monsters well fed, and with another storm brewing in her eyes she said, 'Talking of chaos, have you seen the riverside effect we've got over the road just now? When I took on this job I was of the opinion I'd need skates for the ice, not rubber flippers!'

'Okay, okay, don't lose your hair—it suits you. Come on, let's take a look.'

His unexpected gentleness left Celia without a leg to stand on. Not only had he stopped sounding off to her about his precious gadgets, he was actually offering to accompany her back to the rink to review the position!

Not knowing whether to be mollified or not, she turned and preceded him down the metal stairway Out-. side, the refrigerated vans and lorries were cluttering the forecourt as usual. McCord steered her past a metal fork-lift over-stacked with food cartons and round the damp bulk of a side of beef being transported across her path.

In the rink she was maliciously pleased to see the ice flooding nicely. Now *he* would see that she had just cause for complaint.

McCord's reaction was impossible to fathom. He nodded pleasantly to the staff and even asked old Ibrahim who was sharpening skate blades on the grinding wheel how his wife was.

But the scene on the ice did not indicate a smooth-running concern, Celia noted with renewed satisfaction. The children were seeing who could send up the most spray with their skates, and the *ayahs* looked around and at one another uncertainly, wondering if they should get their young charges dressed and out of the deteriorating conditions.

Black veils were hastily tugged into position as McCord approached. His fluent Arabic and easy manner were devoured by these child-minding and often lonely women. And long before he had finished his lengthy chat, the dark eyes above the veils were smiling at him coyly.

The children had clustered around him at the edge of the ice, and to her disgust Celia discovered that instead of being the ogre of the situation he was fast becoming the star attraction. He had a way with children, she had to admit. He transferred his attention to them as suavely as he had just a moment ago given it all to the ladies, and what he said kept the tots' piquant gazes riveted on him, evoking a titter here, a giggle there, and a squirm of bright-eyed laughter from the older end.

Tiny Maryam, in candy-floss organdy was moved to show off with a charming pirouette, and McCord demonstrated his approval by swinging her up into his arms and allowing small arms to wind lovingly round his neck. Strong, even teeth, just less than white, gave his smile a masculine appeal; something the *ayahs* were not slow to appreciate, judging by the reserved sparkle atop the veils.

Ahmad and young Husain clowned before him as he talked, and left in the dark because of her ignorance of Arabic, Celia asked distrustfully, 'What are you telling them?'

'I'm just apologising for the poor quality of the ice,' he shrugged, 'and explaining that we're doing all we can to put matters right.'

She looked at her watch and seeing that it was only ten minutes to closing time she left him with a dry, 'Well, I'm glad someone appreciates your particular brand of fiction!'

After lunch and a lie down at the hotel, Celia went for her usual hour to the pool. Too hot for anything else at this time of day, she had the choice of drifting irresolutely in the air-conditioned comfort of her suite, or splashing in the sparkling water surrounded by shady palms. She had long ago plumped for the latter as a pleasant way of spending the lengthy break between morning and afternoon sessions.

But today she moved languidly through the half-deserted gardens, a fluttering restlessness inside her, the aftermath of her clash with McCord this morning. There was something in that embrace of his in the compressor room that seemed branded on her mind, and though she saw no sense in reliving those heart-thudding moments, she had no real desire to erase them from her thoughts.

Splashing in the pool would help, she decided, and she did three brisk lengths of the pool as a start to her programme. It was when she was emerging dripping from another cooling bout later that the towel she had been about to reach for from her table under the palms was dropped around her shoulders by unseen hands. Startled, she turned and was rocked further to find herself looking up into the same blue eyes which had caused her considerable mental torment this past hour or so.

McCord here! Her surprise must have shown in her

face, for, leisurely arranging the soaking, flaxen strands
of her hair over the towel, he said easily, 'Relax. I
haven't come in a working capacity. At least, only to
say that I'm closing the rink for the rest of the day.'

Celia was conscious of the world becoming hazy with
his appearance; of the sprinkling of guests around the
pool suddenly receding beyond the haze so that her own
little area beneath the palm was like an island of uncer-
tainty with his fingers arranging the tendrils of her hair.

'Don't tell me,' she tried to sound flippant, 'that
you're actually giving me the day off?'

'I've no choice,' he slanted her a begrudging gleam.
'The ice is going to get worse rather than better. But
freezing conditions are improving at the plant and after
a close down for a couple of days you'll be getting all
the pressure you need at the rink.'

Celia sat down in her chair, droplets glistening on her
smooth, lightly tanned skin, her brilliant cornflower blue
swimsuit still wet. But she needed support for her legs
for some inexplicable reason. McCord looked overwhelmingly unbusinesslike in grey slacks and pale
checked sports shirt. He had ordered himself a drink,
she saw, picking up her own glass, a social touch which
left her slightly out of her depth.

'You couldn't be suggesting,' she said over the top of
her glass,' a *two-day* break? . . . But wait a minute . . .'
Something had just slotted into her mind. 'Tomorrow
. . . isn't that the public holiday I've been hearing about?'
It was. She remembered now. And if the rink was to be
closed for the rest of the day, that meant she wouldn't
see Tariq tonight. And they had made no firm arrangements for their date tomorrow, and Kuwait.

'That's right.' McCord was watching her lazily as he
replied. 'It seems the ideal time, don't you agree, to leave
the ice in suspension until we're back to full pressure
again?'

'Oh yes.' Quickly she replied while her mind was
rapidly coming round to the realisation that with the

Alhambra all locked up for the evening there would be no way of getting in touch with Tariq.

Contrary to her own secret dilemma McCord seemed well pleased with his plan. He lay back in his chair and pulled on his drink, though his gaze on her, intensely blue in the outdoors and fainly hooded, was offputting to say the least when she madly wanted to pursue her own thoughts.

'I ought to point out,' he put in, after idly removing his glance to view the scene of bathers and loungers around the pool, 'that tomorrow will not be entirely a work-free day.'

Celia bristled. 'I might have known! A public holiday, only I don't happen to be a member of the public, is that right——?'

'Let me finish——' His smile was not exactly soothing. 'You're forgetting the one other occupation, aren't you? That of finding your long-lost mother substitute, Nevine.'

Celia blinked. To be truthful she *had* forgotten. At least since McCord had unsettled her with his presence at the pool.

While she was dumbly admitting this he went on, making no effort to keep a slightly sanctimonious note out of his voice, 'As you've given so much of your time to the smooth running of the Alhambra, I consider it only fair to devote a little of my time in assisting you with the job you originally came to Bahrain to do. I think I'm right in assuming that you haven't yet spread your net to the adjoining Banabba islands, so I suggest we take a boat there in the morning and try our luck.'

Celia's eyes, silvered by the sunlight, became round. This was a side of McCord she hadn't come across; not since the early days when he had taken her to the soirée and dinner party at Rifaa for the purposes of asking around. Suppressing an urge to enthuse, she viewed him instead with ironical disbelief. 'The great McCord offering to leave all his pet projects unattended? Actually

shelving the pressing call of business for the more frivolous pastime of joining in a missing persons hunt!'

His look was one of mocking regret. 'Maybe I'll do
some business in the Banabba Islands. We'll be going
on one of the native dhows, by the way,' he added. 'I
own a couple, and one of them, the *Sea Roc*, is in harbour at the moment.'

Celia's expression now matched the delighted in-
credulity in her eyes. 'One of those camel-necked craft
with the big rust-red sails and everything. I don't believe
it!'

'Be ready at nine in the morning,' he said with an
indulgent gleam,' and we'll pretend we're doing a pirate
run.'

She laughed, struck with the idea, but was sufficiently
down to earth to make the wicked observation, 'The
usual office hours, of course.'

'Sailing's a leisurely business.' Amused, McCord
didn't deny that he was a man who normally made every
minute count. 'The earlier we start the more ground we
get to cover in the time allotted.'

Celia couldn't imagine floating round the Persian Gulf
with a man like McCord, engaged in a search, that was,
to say the least, far out of his usual realm of operations.
But that didn't dilute the tiny thrill of pleasure that was
rapidly flowering within her at the thought.

Relaxed now, she sipped at her drink, only to find
McCord finishing his off with one gulp after a glance at
his wrist watch. He rose, towering momentarily, and
gave her a brief salute. 'Okay, see you tomorrow. Enjoy
the rest of your day, Miss Darwell.'

'Thank you, I intend to, Mr McCord.' She showed
her teeth in a smile that was not meant to broadcast her
irritation. Here she was, just coming round to the idea
of lingeringly plying him with questions about tomorrow
and generally sunning herself, not only in the Bahrainian
warmth but in his unaccustomed conciliatory company,
when he upped with that all too familiar preoccupied

look on his face and smilingly left her flat.

She watched him go with more than a little curiosity. Just what would be the reason for that fleeting look of concern that had passed across his features just now? Something to do with the pressure of business? She didn't think so. He was not dressed for ice-engineering duties, or high-powered technical chat. But what else was there in his work-packed life? Wondering, she gave up after a while and returned to the rosy prospect of staying by the pool the whole afternoon and later taking as long as she liked over dinner in the luxurious ambience of the hotel restaurant.

CHAPTER EIGHT

IT wasn't until Celia was lying betweeen the sheets after deciding on an early night in preparation for the morrow that it occurred to her to remember Tariq, and then only as a sleepy afterthought. As he was not in the habit of appearing until the latter half of the evening session he would have arrived at the rink only a short while ago to find it all shuttered up. Too late for him to do anything about confirming the plans he'd had in mind.

She was ready long before the stipulated hour next morning. Always an earlier riser, she loved to witness the day's emergence in a saffron flush which gave the sea the appearance of oiled silk and the island a mystic quality as it rose from the deliciously cooling vapours left over from the night.

Though she supposed she ought to dress for sailing, Celia baulked at the idea of wearing slacks yet again on this, one of her rare days off. So it was in flowered sundress and dainty-heeled sandals that she took up her vantage point in the hotel lobby. Even at this hour the place was crowded, with the usual travelling salesmen, oil personnel and freelance agents dealing in everything from washing machines to private jets. Men in Dacron suits and others more indifferently attired kept their ears tuned for easy pickings that might come their way in the non-stop buzz of gossip.

Celia felt somewhat swamped by the atmosphere, though she had acquired a veneer now against the openly interested glances, and the more blatant ones of out-and-out seduction. McCord, when he arrived, showed some distaste at finding her here, a slender brown and gold figure in fragile cotton. He fished her

from the masculine mêlée and was just about to steer
her to the outdoors when an arm came to rest heavily
around his shoulder and the slurred speech of its owner
sounded in their ears. 'Well, if it ishn't my old mate
McCord!'

'Mike!' With something like surprised exasperation in
his voice McCord gripped the man's arm. 'Do you realise I've been searching the whole damn town for you?
For the love of——' he let a curse go under his breath.
'It looks as if you've been here all night, and drinking
too!'

'While 'Mike', a thick-set individual in his late fifties,
continued to slump, giving Celia a moon-faced smile,
McCord said to her, supporting the man's full weight,
'Sorry, but I'm going to have to take him home. He's
due at the oilfields at two for a pretty important operation, and there'll be the devil to pay if he's not on the
job this time.'

Mike had started to snore happily and showing her
concern Celia asked, 'Is there anything I can do?'

McCord thought about it, making clumsily for the
outdoors, and nodded. 'We'll take your car. I'll sit in
the back to see that the lovable old soak comes to no
harm.'

Celia soon saw that he was speaking from experience,
for they hadn't been on the road long before Mike leapt
up from his slumber like a mad elephant, battling at the
doors and windows in a rollicking attempt to find out
where he was. When McCord had calmed him and his
musical snores were all she had to contend with she was
able to make more headway following the directions that
would bring them to their passenger's house.

Surprisingly for an oil man, he didn't live on one of
the estates provided but in the heart, it seemed, of
Manama itself. She turned right, and right again
through streets of crumbling mud walls and latticed
balconies. Labyrinths, she supposed was what the desert
people called these mazes they had constructed for

themselves centuries ago.

At the heart of this maze they came to Mike's house. They searched for his key and got him indoors. Celia saw whitewashed rooms, also labyrinthine in design it seemed, with hanging lamps and threadbare Persian carpets. The room they were in most of the others appeared to open on to a half-covered courtyard where the breeze wafted the scents of a eucalyptus tree and other greenery.

McCord eased his lifeless burden into a chair. He had obviously decided against getting him to bed, and Celia could guess why. 'Coffee,' he said. 'We need lots of black coffee.'

'Let me do it.' She looked around for the kitchen.

'Through here.' He led her across the courtyard to a low-ceilinged space pungent with the aroma of hanging herbs. He helped her to locate the things she would need, the two of them brushing close in the small area lined with rough wooden cupboards and shelves. Celia wanted to smile, but refrained from doing so because of the apparent gravity of the situation. The sight of McCord pottering with saucepans and supply canisters in the crude domesticity of their surroundings was somehow highly amusing.

He went back across the courtyard and she could hear him working at rousing the recumbent figure with sharp talk. From what she could make out from the snatches of conversation she caught as she made the coffee, this lapse of Mike's was one of many in the past, and as he was a top man at the oilfield it was debatable how long he was going to be able to hold down his job if they continued.

She could find only a tin mug to hold the coffee. Testing it for coolness, she took it into the whitewashed room and waited for the appropriate moment to get some inside the man.

Some progress had been made, for his eyes were open and registering a vague awareness of what was going on, though his face still wore the rosy hue of too much liquor. It was a good face, mature, with kindly lines; not one that belonged to a confirmed drunk, Celia felt. Viewing it clearly for the first time, she had the oddest sensation that she had seen it somewhere before. Something about the eyes ... or was it the smile? ... Tantalisingly the memory eluded her ...

'Come on, snap out of it, Mike!' McCord slapped the man's face with grim affection. 'You've got what's left of the morning to shake off the booze and make like an oil company exec. And if I see you sinking this low **again** I'm gonna have your ears, understand!'

'Awsh, McCord ... you are the doggonest ... shlavedriver ...'

'You love your work. Now quit making out you want to commit professional suicide and think about the guys who are depending on you out there.'

At a sign Celia stepped forward with the mug of coffee. She was prepared to have a go at tipping it into the slack mouth, but McCord took it from her with a look that said she was to keep clear and began the operation himself.

She went for more coffee ... and more and within an hour they had Mike sitting up straight if a little mystified, and halfway on the road to recovery. McCord began to relax. He even gave Celia a comradely smile. She felt curiously touched, perhaps because they had both worked so hard and fatigue was making her sentimental.

'I've a feeling we're going to do it,' he said, straightening from the constant necessity of cajoling Mike from his stupor. 'But I want to be sure that he gets to the oilfield with no mishaps. Do you think you'll be okay if I slip out and make a phone call?'

'Of course,' Celia nodded. 'Should I keep up with the black coffee?'

'All you can manage.' He looked grateful. 'I'll get one of my men to take over here when we go, and see that Mike gets to work on time.'

He went out quickly, disappearing along the alley, and Celia turned back to keeping an eye on the cheerful hulk in the chair. He had taken to singing snatches of American ballads in between making firm efforts to appear sober. Celia suppressed a smile. It was impossible not to like this friend of McCords, for all his unmanly state at the moment. That he *was* a man of decent morals and firm ideals she felt instinctively, and looking at him while she applied the mug to his lips she wondered about the tinge of sadness that was creeping into his countenance in the wake of the receding euphoria of drink; an habitual melancholy, she would have said, judging by the deep lines scored in the well-moulded features.

It was gratifying to see him showing a lucid interest in his surroundings at last, though he clung to the last vestiges of drunkenness with slurred snatches of song as though reluctant to face the harsher world of sobriety.

Celia reckoned that one more dose of coffee would do the trick. Looming in, she had got quite adept at feeding Mike like an overgrown baby. This time, when a kind of blank recognition showed in his eyes, she supposed it was because he was becoming used to her administrations. Then suddenly he acted completely out of character by gripping her round the waist with both arms and tightening them so that the mug was suspended giddily in space over one big shoulder.

Helpless, she heard the sob that crumpled his face and burying it against her he cried, 'Mandy!—You here? Why didn't you say—why didn't someone tell me? . . . Aw, Mandy . . . I didn't want you . . . to see me . . . like this . . .'

Mandy! Celia was transfixed. Not only because she couldn't move a muscle in the bear hug, but also because something had just clicked into place. The round, sunny features of this man and those in the photograph over the desk in McCord's office at the rink! There was no time to do more than glimpse the possibility, for the man whose arms imprisoned her had risen and they were swaying unsteadily like a couple of drunks.

Afraid that they were going to go crashing over, Celia tried a soothing tone. 'You're making a mistake, Mike. *I'm* not Mandy. I'm Celia Darwell ... I work for McCord ... we've been trying to get you on your feet for——'

'Aw, Mandy, ya should've said ... ya should've told me ... Look at me ... your gin-soaked old man ... and you purty as a picture ...' Obsessed as he was with a feeling of disgrace, the sobs were those of a man making the traumatic withdrawal from the bounds of intoxication.

But knowing this didn't help Celia. She was locked against his shuddering frame and was beginning to feel about as efficient as a rag doll in helping him over the rough going. The coffee mug crashed to the ground and the sharp corner of some jutting piece of furniture dug into her back as she fought the losing battle to keep them both upright. Overcome with shame and remorse, her captor seemed bent on proffering his apologies with the ever-increasing stranglehold of a love-hug that was plagued with unsteadiness.

About thirteen stone of brawn and brute force levelled against the solar plexus didn't make for easy breathing, and a feeling of faintness warned Celia that struggling would only aggravate her position. She had resigned herself to waltzing in this macabre fashion until one of them caved in when a sharp voice pierced the rushing in her ears. 'Mike! What the hell's got into you?'

McCord! Thank heavens he was back. He strode across the room, an action which only served to tighten the grip of the thick arms around her, if this were possible. 'Mandy!—Mandy!—All I've got ... all I've got in the world ...!'

There was something tear-jerking in this semi-comatose baring of the soul. But McCord was anything but dewy-eyed. 'Get back in the chair, old son,' his voice was harsh with rebuke. 'I'm disappointed to find I can't leave you in the company of a lady for five minutes without——'

Mike reacted like a wild bull at the intrusion. 'Nobody comes between me and my li'l girl!'

'I wouldn't dream of it, Mike,' McCord began to extricate Celia from the elephantine grip with a hard smile. 'But this happens to be Miss Darwell, an employee of mine, and if you don't snap out of your daydreams I'm going to have to give you an unfriendly punch on the jaw!'

Something about his steely attitude must have got through to the befogged brain, for with a laugh of bravado which didn't quite mask another rending sob Mike reeled away and landed with unsteady precision back in his chair.

Celia was making good use of McCord's support, for the simple fact that the abrupt release from the tourniquet hold on her had sent the blood rushing to her head in a blinding pain.

'Are you okay?' McCord steadied her against him, feeling the trembling that Celia would have given anything to hold in check.

'I . . . think so,' she gave a shaky laugh. 'I'd hate to know the force of Mike's wholehearted affection!'

'Rest a while.' McCord eased her head against his shoulder, and as he kept an eye on the half-dozing figure in the chair he said, 'Drink does funny things to a man. Such behaviour is totally alien to Mike's nature in normal circumstances.'

'Is he . . . Mandy's father?' Celia ventured to ask.

McCord nodded. 'Michael Forbes Bennet. He's got a responsible position at the oilfields. It's been his life's work, and with his retirement to think of and a pension that's going to make him very comfortably off, he can't afford to mess things up at this stage.'

'Why should he want to do that?' Celia wondered aloud.

'That's the hell of it, I don't think he does.' McCord sighed heavily. 'His wife died fifteen months ago. He's taken it hard; sold up all he had—a smart villa over at Juffant among other things—and dug himself in here where he lives like a recluse apart from the stints he does at the oilfields. And these are becoming somewhat irregular, due to his penchant lately for turning to the bottle for release.'

Celia said, 'It upset him when he thought his daughter had paid him a visit, but why should it do that? Surely she would be a great help to him at a time like this.'

McCord shook his head. 'Mike's a proud man. Until he's got a grip on himself and learned to cope with reality, he'd rather Mandy stayed away.'

Yes, Celia had seen some of that pride showing even through the disfigurement of drunkenness. Her cheek lay against McCord's chest. She felt calmed in his embrace. And all at once the knowledge that Mike didn't want his daughter in Bahrain was somehow an infinitely comforting thought.

She and McCord ended up having lunch with Mike. As Celia pointed out, he ought to have something inside him before going off to work, to combat the after-effects of alcohol. And once she had convinced McCord that she had suffered no real harm while he had been out of the house, he agreed it was a good idea. The only driver he'd been able to locate on the phone who was not out of town still had a refrigerated load to deliver across the causeway to Muharraq before he could come and pick Mike up for the oilfield, so there was time enough to arrange some sort of meal for him.

They rooted in the small kitchen together, McCord huge in yachting shirt and sailcloth slacks tossing out what he could find from the sparse food store. Celia found a linen kitchen apron for the front of her dress and for the three of them she concocted a spread of bacon, egg and mushrooms, and segments of mandarins which McCord plucked from a tree in the courtyard.

It was really a very masculine meal, with hunks of American-baked bread which Celia cut purposely for the men, guessing that this was Mike's usual style of eating, with probably every meal coming out of the frying pan.

He had washed and changed before sitting down at the table and though he said little, preferring to coast along on the memory of an all-night binge, Celia felt that they could congratulate themselves that they had once again made an oil official of him. Frequently she met McCord's blue glance across the table or when they were making trips to and from the kitchen across the courtyard, and his bemused light at their joint domestic role, together with something else she couldn't quite fathom, added to her lighthearted feel.

The driver came just when the two of them were doing the dishes. They saw Mike into the car. 'You've got chauffeur service today, you old trouble-shooter,' McCord put an arm around the thick-set shoulders. 'And good luck with the top brass inspection this afternoon.'

'I'll soon put them in their place,' came the confident reply. 'And McCord—' Mike looked towards the doorway from his open window, '—thanks.'

Celia knew that shyly he had included her in his gratitude, and with McCord she waved affectionately until the car was lost in the maze of alleys.

It was something of an anticlimax when they turned back indoors. And not only that, but being alone with McCord in a tiny mud dwelling which had its charm for all its masculine bareness was considerably different from being alone with him in the clinically businesslike surroundings of the office at the ice rink. It had to be, didn't it? with them bumping into each other as they replaced washed pans and items of crockery.

Celia would have been able to breathe a lot easier if he had gone to put his feet up like any other man, but though this was not his natural habitat, obviously, he seemed to derive a certain amount of lazy contentment in handing her the things she needed, or removing those which she discarded.

With feminine consciensciousness Celia felt that they should leave everything as they had found it. In fact, the little living room and kitchen were spotless when she had finished, a state of affairs considerably improved since their entry.

Eyeing her satisfied expression, McCord handed her her handbag from where she had dropped it on a chair and drawled, 'Ready for the boat trip now?'

'Can we still go?' Her heart leapt. Having spent half the day with Mike she had assumed that the outing was off.

'I told the *nakoda*—or skipper to you—we'd be held up.' He escorted her to the door. 'The *Sea Roc's* in the harbour, waiting for us to show up.'

Celia felt a new zest in his words. She had combed her hair and generally freshened up in the little bathroom, and with the whole afternoon before them it truly felt like a holiday.

McCord locked the door and put the key high up in a nearby window-nook. 'A little secret of Mike's,' he grinned. 'Though he could leave the door open here and nobody would touch a thing.'

'Do they still chop hands off out here for stealing?' Celia asked with grisly curiosity.

'In some places.' McCord handed her into the car with teasing unconcern, relenting only when her grey eyes widened horrifically to amend it with a laughing, 'But locally I don't think you're likely to see anything but a two-handed populace!'

He drove her car himself to the harbour. Aboard the *Sea Roc* Celia told herself she had to be dreaming. The ballooning red sails seemed to tower above her head and the creaking of its timbers as they rode out to sea gave her the feeling that she and McCord had stepped back a couple of centuries in time.

She wanted to laugh at her nonsense, and half did while viewing turban-clad crewmen in flapping trousers and colourful boleros showing sinewy, teak-skinned arms and chests.

Beside her at the rail McCord watched her changing expressions with lazy amusement. 'Believe it or not,' he said, 'the same sailing craft—roughly in design at least— still ply the Persian Gulf today as they did in the seventeenth century.'

'But with different cargoes, I bet,' Celia smiled, turning to join him in facing seawards.

'Not so different,' he shrugged mysteriously. 'Many still have dubious values—contraband gold, for instance.'

She looked at him to see whether he was joking. 'You don't mean these waters are infested with gold-runners!' And not sure what to make of him she added, 'I hope the *Sea Roc*'s not carrying a hold full of the stuff.'

He laughed. 'If it was it would be on the seabed by now! Gold isn't the lightest of metals to cart around.' He shook his head. 'No, we don't go in for precious cargoes . . . at least, not usually.'

His cryptic gleam as he looked at her made Celia rush on to cover the moment. 'Well, just what are you carrying?'

'If you really want to know I'm afraid it's going to put paid to all those romantic ideas you've been having about our picturesque transport.' He grinned crookedly. 'I have to confess that from the decks downwards the *Sea Roc* is anything but an Arab dhow in the old sense. Her holds are lined and fitted out with the most modern refrigerating equipment, and our cargo, I regret to add, is just mundane packages of frozen foodstuffs.'

Celia gave a shout of laughter. Only McCord would be capable of ruining a perfectly good fairy-tale setting with his ubiquitous freezing methods! As her eyes danced at her thoughts they met his blue laughter and she was a little shaken to find herself on such intimate terms with her boss.

It had all started at Mike's house this morning, and if she wasn't careful she was going to have to come to the conclusion that McCord was not all high-geared businessman.

Gazing seawards after that was less disturbing, and viewing their passage over sun-gilded waters she had to remind herself that this was a semi-working trip. Heavens! She had almost forgotten Nevine and the real reason for this outing.

The scenery was magical. If the *Sea Roc* was pure twentieth century below decks nobody would have known, and under a sky like blue silk, its crystal light intensified by the deep peacock blue of the Gulf waters, the dhow sliced the waves as though commanded by Sinbad himself.

They had to sail southwards down the coast of the main state of Bahrain. From the sea the island seemed suspended in a shimmering veil out of which rose the mosques and minarets and mirage-like skyline of buildings, a disembodied cut-out silvered by the refracted rays of the desert sun.

Out at sea everything was blissfully cool. At this distance the low cliffs and escarpments of the passing coastline, the desolated sand flats with their lonely flights of seabirds were softened by the inner oasis of green and lush palm plantations, like an emerald in a rough pewter setting.

McCord pointed out to her the emergence of the Banabba islands, appearing like strips of desert that had inadvertently found themselves afloat in miles of sea. There were no skylines here, just thorn thickets as they approached and the odd Arab dwelling where scant shade offered some respite from the heat. Celia wondered if there was any point at all in coming this far in search of Nevine, but on arrival she was pleasantly surprised to find the scattering of a fishing community and a sturdy jetty along which the produce they had brought in the holds was soon finding its way on to dry land, transported by waiting refrigerated vans.

McCord had to spend some time generally overseeing the unloading of the stuff for outlying villages, and talking with drivers whose routes covered apparently the adjoining islands as well as this main one of Halab. Celia rested awhile in the cabin McCord had put at her disposal for the trip. Afterwards she bathed her face and arms in deliciously cool water coming from refrigerated supplies (naturally) and scorning make-up now that she had acquired a tan which made her eyes look startlingly grey in contrast, she smoothed her hair, noticing how the sun and sea wind had heightened its dusky barley colour, and went out.

McCord was waiting for her on deck. Judging by his expression he had something on his mind, but he didn't disclose what it was until they were walking along the jetty. Perhaps his idea was that the colourful surroundings of fishing dhows and black-shrouded women would offset her disappointment, for taking her arm he said with a dry grin, 'I'm afraid our trip ashore is going to be purely recreational. I've been checking around and no one in these parts appears to have heard of your Nevine.'

Celia stopped to look at him. She *was* disappointed and not a little puzzled. How could he be so sure when they had yet to set foot on land?

Answering the unspoken question in her eyes, he explained, moving on with her, 'I didn't mention it before, but I gave orders on the *Sea Roc*'s last trip here for each driver to make enquiries along his own route regarding the woman in question. As there are important deliveries to be made—special medical supplies mainly— to every populated spot in these islands you'll gather that they've covered the ground pretty thoroughly, and not one of them has anything to report that might help.'

Celia sighed. 'So Nevine *has* to be in Bahrain itself. It's funny, but that's what I've felt all along.'

'If she's not holed up with some ageing Saudi sheikh; still his favourite dancing girl though running to seed.'

Celia flashed him a look 'It may be a joke to you, but *I* happen to want very much to meet the woman who made such an impact on my father's life.'

'So I've noticed' McCord smiled tightly, his hand still gripping her arm as they walked.

The old discordant relationship was showing signs of surfacing and Celia felt a stab of unhappiness at the trend the conversation had taken. McCord had always shown an open impatience at her desire to turn back the clock thirty years in a land where differing customs made such a feat doubly difficult. Conversely it was *because* she was here in the Middle East and because the life style was so vastly different from her own that Celia felt the need to know the woman whose birthright this was.

She wouldn't expect anyone to understand her mixed up reasoning, least of all McCord, who dealt only with contemporary Bahrain and its new crop of business-men.

'The sun will be down in half an hour.' He handed her into the air-conditioned interior of a small car obviously waiting there for his use. 'Meanwhile we'll tour the sights. What there are,' he added with morose humour.

The scenery seemed to match their mood at the moment; a rapid deterioration, Celia was sad to note, from the one in which they had started out earlier. How was it possible, she wondered, for the atmosphere to cloud over with such speed when only a moment before all had been smooth?

CHAPTER NINE

CELIA gave her attention to the views, as bleak as her thoughts. They had left the pocket of activity at the jetty and now there was nothing but a rough shoreline and a dusty mud village in the distance. Feeling that some comment was expected of her, Celia asked, 'How on earth do the inhabitants survive, marooned in a place like this? There doesn't appear to be any industry apart from the boats.'

McCord shrugged. 'Since the palmy days of pearl fishing there's nothing much to keep anyone here. Your guess is as good as mine what they do with their time, or how they make it pay.'

'Pearl fishing!' The very sound of this, the most romantic of occupations, lightened the atmosphere fractionally and Celia, bent on pursuing it, suggested brightly, 'Perhaps it still pays in a small way in these parts, even today.'

'I wouldn't be surprised.' McCord was noncommittal, much to her mild exasperation. He probably knew to the last man what they did locally, but for some reason was not going to expand. However, he did enlarge on the pearling industry generally, and as they crawled, as a way of passing the time, beside the lacy surf of the sea's edge, she listened fascinated.

'It may sound colourful, but it's always been a tough way of making a living,' McCord told her. 'Less than one third of every catch in the old days produced pearls of any value. You could say that the entire Gulf fleet never contributed to more than a couple of the type of necklaces seen on the Edwardian women of the day, in one season.'

134

'Can one find pearl oysters just anywhere in these waters?' Celia asked.

'Not usually.' McCord avoided a pile of fish traps at the side of the track. 'Oyster beds shift with the tides or after a certain period of time. Sometimes they yield a harvest of good market value. On the other hand, banks have been known to be sterile for years. None of them are charted. The *nakhoda*, the skipper of each craft, has his own theories on where the best pickings are, and what he knows he keeps to himself. These are trade secrets handed down in families.'

Celia mused on this and said with a dreamy smile, 'I wonder if Tariq knows any of these trade secrets? I bet he does.'

'Tariq?' McCord's smile had a faint twist to it. But Celia was too taken up with her own ponderings to notice. It came to her with a mild shock that she hadn't given a thought to the likeable young Arab all day, or felt the slightest compunction at leaving him high and dry when they had had a kind of loose arrangement to spend the day together.

After but a fleeting twinge she said lightly, 'Of course! He's bound to have some idea of where the productive beds are to be found, even to this day, as he's descended from a pearl merchant family. He knows a lot about them. He once told me that his grandfather—or whoever it was—believed that the finest and densest white pearls came from deep water, and those tinted with colour were shallow water yields.' Celia gave a small laugh. 'Although I'll admit Tariq is the least likely of pearl fishers!'

'Why do you say that?' McCord's taut smile lingered.

As far as Celia was concerned the question was superfluous. 'Can you imagine the sophisticated Tariq in ragged turban and swimming dhoti poised on the bow of a pearling dhow?' she said with amusement.

McCord kept his gaze on the rough route. 'Would he appeal to you in that guise?' he asked lazily.

'Appeal to *me*?' Celia was floored by the question. But considering, she laughed. 'I have to admit, no. Despite all my romantic notions about the East I like Tariq as he is. His Westernised business air and mode of dress suits him, although he does have a kind of dashing charm when he puts on one of these burnous things that he sometimes wears, don't you think?'

'I wouldn't know.' McCord brough the car to a stop in the village and clamped on the brakes. 'It takes a woman's eyes to fantasise. A man only sees fact.'

'What a dull time you all must have!' Celia carped, aware by the grip on her arm as he helped her from the car that the conversation had done nothing to ease the antagonistic mood that persisted between them.

However, the scant increase in scenic detail created a diversion. The mud village fronted the beach where goats scavenged among the fish traps. White donkeys idled outside some of the dwellings like privileged members of the family and black-shrouded Arab women busy with outside chores dropped everything like so many black beetles scuttling for cover when they saw McCord's masculine figure approaching.

But there was one dwelling where the reception was different. An elderly Arab almost as tall as McCord emerged from the interior, and though he was roughly clad; he had something of a village-head authority about him. He clasped McCord's hand in his own sun and sea-weathered mahogany one and the two men greeted each other warmly in Arabic.

'Mahmoud is a friend of mine.' McCord drew Celia forward to introduce her to the headman. 'There's nothing he doesn't know about transport in the Gulf. He proved a great help when I was buying the two dhows I own now.'

Though the women of the household had beaten a hasty retreat they were sternly commanded to provide tokens of hospitality for the guests, and rugs and cushions were brought out and arranged with shifty movements beside the doorway where a cool pitcher of goat's milk and rough goblets had been placed on a low stand, itself centred on a ceremonial remnant of tattered carpet.

Traditionally the men sat to one side discussing trade and local commercial trends—at least that was what Celia presumed, as all Arabs appeared to have an avid interest in these topics. For herself she was glad of some small respite from the overpowering effect of McCord's company. It wasn't as though they had said or done a lot since leaving Manama at lunch time, and yet she felt curiously drained as though she had been battling with some unseen force that at times had threatened to carry her along on wings and now fomented the air between them.

But for the moment, with cushions at her back against the cool wall of the mud dwelling, she felt strangely rested. In the silvered light of dusk the sea mirrored the tranquil opaque sky and the sable masts of fishing craft, and distant dhows were stencilled against the fading brightness of day. Her nostrils caught the clean scent of the sea's waft before it was lost in the exuding warmth and distinct odour of the Arab village.

As the shadows lengthened she relaxed, watching where the men sat conversing in rapid Arabic, McCord's less than white smile stirring her in an odd way. She wondered about him, about his younger days, and what it was that had led him to carve a life for himself out here in the Middle East. But these were questions one didn't ask a man like McCord. His eyes were wont to reflect his ice-like approach both to life as well as his profession, although of late when he had looked at her ... She shrugged mentally. The slight thawing could only mean that he found her a useful component in the workings of his complex business schemes.

In crude lighting the evening meal of the Arab household was served as appeared to be customary out of doors. The women didn't eat in McCord's presence, but as faceless bundles they bustled out with cooking pots and serving dishes, departing with phantom speed when all was prepared. Celia was left to cope as the *infidel* she was in the added masculine presence of sons and nephews who had come home after a days work at the harbour. Seated at the low table, she had the sinking feeling that she was going to be swamped in the lusty exchanges delivered in the local tongue. But then a pleasant surprise came her way, for Ismael, the oldest son of the household, had heard McCord introducing her in English and below the harsh babble of his relatives he tried a few broken sentences of the half-forgotten language.

'Once I work for oil peoples in Iran,' he told her. 'But it is not my like. The ... this how you say with the nose? ... *afwan*, the smell. Ugh! I think that to its compare fish is not so bad.'

Ismael had a big black beard and a wicked sense of humour which didn't go at all with the biblical air he evoked in rough robes. His relatives looked on, envious of his ability to bring a smile to Celia's lips and sometimes shy laughter. McCord gave her an enigmatic look during the meal, though she was doing nothing but politely satisfying a healthy hunger with the food which, despite its strangeness, was good. While he was looking at her she had a better view than he had of Mahmoud, the head of the household, whose eyes, twinkling greatly, were musing on McCord's preoccupation with his son Ismael rather than the food.

There were cinammon squares, poppyseed bonbons and almond cakes to round off the meal; delicacies whipped up at a moment's notice by the servile black bundles, Celia suspected. And as an added honour to the guests Mahmoud brought out a bottle of Pharaoh's wine from his hoard of foreign treasures, reserved for such occasions.

As their religion forbade the drinking of wine, it was Celia and McCord alone who clinked glasses; an oddly intimate gesture amidst the noisy approval of the masculine audience.

The electric blue of the sky and the yellow glow from the crude lamps lit the friendly faces of the Mahmoud Ali Mirza family as Celia and McCord finally took their leave. She shook Ismael's big hand demurely and the rest of his brothers and cousins lined up—some eight or nine of them—to indulge at least in this one Western custom. Her hand somewhat bruised, Celia turned laughingly last of all to Mahmoud, who gave her the old-fashioned salaam instead, but his eyes were gentle and musing and he wished her well, she was sure, in his softly spoken Arabic as she joined up with McCord for the walk back to the car.

She felt that those wise, twinkling eyes followed the two of them for long enough before turning back to the house glow and family matters.

On the ride back to the jetty McCord said with his McCord smile, 'You made a hit with Ismael.'

'His English was hilarious, but he was so nice and unaffected I couldn't let him see that I was amused at anything but his jokes,' said Celia with a comical expression.

It was lost on McCord, whose eyes glinted out into the night.

The *Sea Roc*, its loading and unloading completed, was waiting to set sail when they arrived. On deck later Celia felt choked at the beauty of the evening, the turquoise radiance of the night sky silhouetting the glamorous lines of their transport, the sea like black satin beneath them, reflecting stars that were like dancing fireflies on the heaving calm. It was warmer now than it had been earlier with the sparkling sea-winds, but it was a velvet caress on the skin, made pleasant by nocturnal breezes singing close to the waves.

Celia thought she would die with the exquisite pain of witnessing such beauty—a ridiculous frame of mind, she told herself wryly when McCord was standing beside her at the rail with hardly a look of appreciation on his face. Or at least maybe he was aware of the magic but preferred his usual phlegmatic approach to it all. No, that wasn't right either. Celia gave up trying to analyse the man at her side. She had been doing it most of the afternoon and finding herself deeper in a mesh of irritations and uncertainties at his nearness.

He was the first to speak when they had been sailing for a good twenty minutes, and by the sound of it they might well have been back at the dark beach side, for his opening words were still linked with the brief conversation that had taken place in the car.

'I can see the wisdom of the Arabs in keeping their women segregated,' his steely reflections were delivered more to the ocean than to her. 'Males of any creed tend to be males when exposed to their mating opposites.'

Celia felt the familiar knot of unease burgeoning in her as she replied tensely, 'We don't all regard our opposite numbers as mating potentials. It is possible to have entertaining conversation with the opposite sex without giving the gender a thought.'

'Like you and Ismael, for instance?' McCord's tones were hardened and sardonic. 'You've got to be naïve if you didn't notice the way he looked at you with those "entertaining" black eyes of his.'

'As a matter of fact I did,' Celia felt moved to reply. 'But it does make a change, once in a while, to be treated as something other than a useful fixture in a working combine.' She didn't know why she had come out with that. It was not what she had intended to say. Not at all.

McCord's smile was goadingly masculine. 'The Arabs are never likely to see a woman anyway but for what she's intended.'

Celia felt her cheeks flame. 'Your opinion of them in this field is so low I wonder you've been able to put up with them all these years,' she flung at him. 'Or is it because you're a male yourself you can ride this lamentable fluke in their character?'

'It has its advantages being a man in a place like this.'

'Of course, a man will see that it has!' she was not slow to retort, hinting with distaste at his own party habits where there was no shortage of feminine partners. 'While the womenfolk are expected to remain tucked away in the background, serving useful purposes like back-breaking house labourers, and passive bed-mates. Well, that might be fine for the men here, but if I were one of their ladies I wouldn't stick it for five minutes.'

'The passive bed-mate bit . . . or the back-breaking chores?' McCord had turned her way and his eyes were lit with a mixture of steely humour and stringent amusement.

'You can laugh if you like.' Celia lifted her chin at him. 'Suffice to say I have no intention of donning the black robe of submission while I'm in Bahrain. As far as I'm concerned the unattached Bahrainis are every bit as entertaining as any Englishman, and as there's no law against it I shall have as many Arab friends as I like.' She felt breathless after her self-assertive splurge. She had started off defending the downtrodden Arab woman and somehow ended up flaunting the emancipation of her own kind.

It was an attitude that McCord was in no mood to tolerate. He grabbed her suddenly in a hold that transmitted something of the fury of his gaze with its roughness. 'That's fighting talk,' his smile had a grim curl to it, 'when you think you came pretty close to being landed with an Arab for the rest of your life.'

Kamel! Oh yes, it was obvious where his thoughts lay.

'I was a beginner then,' she tried to shake off his hold, 'But you can rest assured I know my way around now.'

His answer to this was to wrench her close to him so that her feet barely touched the ground. 'While you're under my protection,' he ground out, 'you'll comport yourself like a decent British expatriate. And any talk will be the friendly kind and nothing else.'

'I told you once before, McCord, you don't own me!' Celia was quivering at these petty bickering exchanges. It was both laughable and excruciatingly tearful to find oneself saying the first crazy thing that came into one's head. How, she wanted to know, had they got into this emotional upheaval? It was like a giant force that certainly didn't come from the ultra-calm of the Gulf waters, but its spell was such that she felt helpless in its momentum.

'No, but I own your time, or most of it.' McCord's darkened gaze blazed down at her. 'And you'll tread carefully where the Arabs are concerned. That's an order from me.'

All this because Ismael had looked at her in an over-friendly fashion! What did he think? That every encounter was going to be another Kamel? It was true she had warily been of that opinion herself once, but, hardly in the mood to admit this now, she flashed. 'I'm not one of your ice-boxes! There's a little more to me than frosted wiring and obedient switches!'

While his face was dark with some inner emotion at her self-willed obstinacy there was a twitch of bemusement around his mouth as he held her panting frame against him. 'Nevertheless,' he bit out, 'you will do as I say and keep clear of the womanising Arabs.'

'I'll do as I please!' Angry breath mingling with angry breath. Celia was reminded of another time, another place—the compressor room at McCord's freezing plant. Was it only yesterday that they had collided head-on, with the same mouth to mouth, body to body clash of wills? Tonight's episode had spiralled out of petty disagreemements that were too stupid to recall, but there was a matching choking defiance on her side and the same odd-lit determination on his.

How would it end? Celia had no intention of capitu-lating this time. There was no lever now that McCord could wrench her from with his brute force. But it was odd too how that same suspended feel froze the moment.

Above her pounding heart she wanted to laugh bitterly at her choice of adjectives. Could anything be more apt where McCord was concerned? ... although less ice-like she had never seen him. In fact there was a molten look in his eyes dominating her view now.

Rebellion in every quivering part of her, she matched fire for fire there, then suddenly the moment exploded with his mouth crashing down on hers.

Celia was stunned like a trapped bird. But it was a rosy kind of imprisonment, for a radiance out-glowing angry sparks spread through her, travelling along her veins like quicksilver at McCord's touch. McCord! How often had she wondered what his party partners experienced in his arms? McCord! Who was not just any man when it came to driving his point home, she had long since suspected, and was now patently convinced.

His kiss was fierce, his embrace relentless, and while she inwardly cursed the puniness of her woman's frame, something sang secretly somewhere, the joys of knowing such an affliction. Her thoughts driving out all opposition, she *was* in danger of surrendering; dizzily, drowningly in danger of giving herself to those savagely demanding lips, to his arms which strained her so close she felt almost a part of his being. Perhaps she did. The urge to give as well as receive was powerfully sweet, and for a moment she became two Celias; one snatching the fruits of clandestine fulfilment, the other fighting to be free of all that was potently desirable.

When she saw the stars again it was to vaguely discover that McCord had raised his head. And just as abruptly, while she was still swaying from the effect, he let her go.

It was some time before she could find her voice, and when she did it sounded quaveringly unreal in her ears. 'Why did you do that?' she demanded, while every part of her cried out for him to do it again.

'For a variety of reasons.' His face was peculiarly in-scrutable in the star glow, as though it had been an out-and-out demonstration that he was the superior being in more than the employer-employee sense of the word. Then he tacked on, 'The main one being that for a long time I've watched you frenziedly digging up the past, trying to unearth a mouldered love when it's your own life you should be thinking of. I just thought I'd give you a sample of what today's living is all about.'

So that was it! She had known all along, of course, that he detested her preoccupation with Nevine and a life long gone, and tightly she replied, 'Frenzied is hardly the word I would apply to a series of dead-ends revealing absolutely nothing of what I came in search for.'

'And that's not surprising,' was his clipped rejoinder. 'When are you going to realise that your father's dead and gone, and that what took place in his lifetime can have little bearing on your own?'

Celia tasted his kiss on her lips and said shakily, 'You've got very odd ways of putting your views across.'

'Would you rather it had been Tariq who woke you up to your own existence as opposed to mooning over your dreams of the past?' he sneered.

They were back to the Arabs again. A favourite theme of his. And Tariq—where did he fit into this discussion?

A pulse hammering in her throat, Celia fired back, 'He might have been less overbearing at the job.'

'Of course, and under the Kuwait stars too!'

Kuwait! How did he know that they had intended to hop a plane in true reckless Arab fashion? She was perplexed, then suddenly the mist cleared and she knew that he had overheard Tariq making the suggestion that night in the shadows of the deserted rink.

Something else hit her then and it was like a boulder bruising her heart as she asked, 'That couldn't be the reason why you suddenly got the urge to forfeit your time to go to the Banabba islands, could it? Tariq and I had a holiday day lined up. But you suddenly came up with other plans; semi-working ones, I seem to recall was how you termed it.'

McCord shrugged, his face shrouded in shadow. 'I did take advantage of the fact that you were work-beholden to me. I like to keep my employees toeing the line wherever possible.'

'In this case, by closing down the rink, so that Tariq was left high and dry without an explanation.'

'As I say, I like to keep a close-circuit watch on all that concerns the smooth running of my particular terrain.'

Celia bit her lip in the shadows, not with anger now, but with a horrible hurt which was stealing over her. The whole day long some part of her had rejoiced at the knowledge that McCord had offered her his services in the search for Nevine—true, he had carried this faithfully through albeit with no results, and even made it something of a memorable occasion—but all the time it had been nothing more than a ruse to outwit Tariq, nothing more than an excuse for McCord to keep her possessively within the bounds of his business domain.

She saw it all now. Ismael ... Kamel ... this heated discussion had all been building up to a showdown over Tariq. And McCord's disapproval of her association with the young Arab whom she had grown to like tremendously over these past weeks even outweighed, she was sure, his dislike of her meddling with the past and Nevine.

The tears filled her eyes, the stupid hurt wouldn't go. But she was not that far gone that she couldn't dig deep for something to fling back. 'You fight dirty, Mr McCord,' she smiled through her tears. 'But then, with your own love life cut up at the moment, your Mandy Bennet, the true star of the show, off the scene as it were, you've got to have your little diversions, I suppose.'

His own mouth twisted, probably at the brightness in her eyes, and harshly he came back with, 'I'll admit life would be a ball if she were around.'

'Well, contrary to your tactics,' she said with brittle exactness, 'you can be sure there'll be no interference from me if that happy day should ever occur.'

'Sore because I messed up your date with Tariq?' His smile was sharp as he looked at her.

'Oh, leave me alone!' She spun away and stumbled below to her cabin, where she stayed for the remainder of the trip. There were more grinding hurts to contend with now, mainly in the shape of Mandy Bennet, and she preferred to come to terms with them on her own.

McCord had made no secret of the fact that he missed the girl whose photograph hung in his office. Why had she, Celia, momentarily let herself assume anything else? It was obvious, wasn't it, that he wouldn't show the concern he did for Mike if he wasn't emotionally involved with the family in some way. And it *was* concern. She knew now that his preoccupation at the hotel pool when he had come to see her yesterday had been for Mike. And when a man goes to the lengths of keeping affectionate tabs on a faltering father, she told herself, as McCord was doing with Michael Bennet, it had to be because he was deeply in love with the daughter.

Celia listened to the creaking timbers and muffled swish of their passage over the waves with a crushing despondency. It had to come some time. McCord, who had never given more than a fraction of himself in the game of love, was now willing to relegate his hard-won professional status and business ambitions to second place for a woman. And that woman was Mandy Bennet.

The *Sea Roc* docked at last and Celia made her own way ashore. Fortunately her car was parked where they had left it on embarking. Wasting no time, she started up and hurtled off alone into the darkness back to the Gulf Hotel.

CHAPTER TEN

McCord had said that she would have no more trouble with the ice, and he was as good as his word. Every day it shone now with the hard, smooth, glass-like surface that is perfect for skate blades.

It was odd not to have anything to complain about. There was no cause for her to go stalking across the alley to the compressor room. And even when she had to go with the valid excuse of seeking McCord's signature for an office chit, it was always to find the regular compressor technician in charge, who would politely tuck the chit into a pocket until the boss called.

But busy as he was with other projects, McCord made his usual unannounced appearances in the ice-rink. Not that Celia, in this case, showed any awareness of his presence. His kiss still burned her lips and would always do in her mind, she knew. As would the knowledge that his fierce embrace had been merely a clinical reminder that one couldn't spend one's time submerged in the past. No, life could be shatteringly overwhelming at first hand, she had discovered.

But she had her work; the children's rehearsals were coming along wonderfully. She also had Tariq's soothing companionship to take her mind off the unsettling McCord. They had quickly sorted out the confusion over the ruptured date. 'I was surprised to find the ice rink all closed up,' Tariq told her, disappointment in his smile as he referred back to that night. 'I called at your hotel the next morning, but they said you were out.'

'McCord felt that he couldn't go on taking the customers' money with the ice as bad as it was,' Celia explained lamely. 'Apparently he regarded the public

147

holiday as strictly a Bahraini affair, so we had a kind of
. . . semi-working day.'

'I shall impose upon you to put matters to rights by
having dinner with me tonight.' There had been humour
in Tariq's dark eyes as he had held her close on the ice.

'I'd like to very much, Tariq,' she had laughed up at
him.

It was a relief to coast along on the undemanding
gentleness of the young Bahraini's nature, after knowing
the forceful, chaotic nearness of McCord, and Celia fell
into the habit of dining with him most evenings, sometimes in the upstairs restaurant, others at some exclusive
spot in town. On these occasions she would bring
something feminine to slip into after work, and they
would leave arm in arm for the outdoors and Tariq's
fabulously expensive motor car.

Part of her knew that she was going all out to show
McCord that she made up her own mind regarding what
company she would keep. But another part of her was
aware that Tariq was dangerously attractive, besides
having a charming and uncomplicated personality.
There was only one hint that unknown currents of passion and feeling flowed beneath the surface of that dark-
eyed serenity, and that was one evening when they had
met to dine at a famed night-spot.

For some reason, perhaps because it went well with
the dress she was wearing, Celia had fastened Kamel's
pendant necklace around her throat.

'What is that?' Tariq spotted it straight away, his dark
eyes hardening as though he recognised it as local mer-
chandise.

'A little gift that one of McCord's employees bought
me . . . oh, quite a while ago.' Celia fingered it lightly.

'Take it off at once! It is cheap and tawdry. I will not
have it tainting your loveliness with its nondescript
value.'

'But, Tariq, it's just a trinket . . . and after all . . .'
With a gesture of impatience he turned her to get at the

fastening himself and afterwards flung the offending
necklace into the gutter with the words, as he guided
her to his car, 'We will see who knows best in the matter
of your adornment.'

She was not wearing a low-necked dress, and apart
from a slight pang when thinking of Kamel's joy in presenting her with it, Celia didn't miss the necklace during
the evening, or for that matter at all. The incident had
completely faded from her mind, only to be vividly unearthed one night in the car when Tariq presented her
with a velvet jewel-case containing the most exquisite
string of pearls she had ever seen.

She sat gazing at them for a full stunned minute
before exclaiming, 'Tariq, they're ... lovely! But I
couldn't possibly wear them. They must be worth a fortune!'

'Were my ancestors not in the pearling business?' he
remarked with a smile that deliberately ignored her perplexed state. 'And you see cleverness runs in the family,
for only pearls of such quality can do justice to the opa-
lescent smoothness of your skin.' He fastened the clasp
under her hair and gazing long at her he said, 'Wear
them for me, Celia. Wear them as a token of our precious friendship and,' he brushed his lips against her
wrist, 'of our growing affection.'

Celia didn't see how she could refuse after that. To
have done so would have hurt Tariq cruelly, she knew.
But it was no easy task to secrete valuable pearls in her
dressing locker at the rink, so that she could don them
for Tariq's benefit later in the evening.

Work and leisure went with a swing. She could even
chat coolly to McCord in Tariq's presence, for the two
men were good friends and neither allowed Celia
to interfere with this; though McCord's eyes when
they met hers had a way of saying things that didn't
match the pleasant words he mouthed, and in
their blue depths she was conscious of a kind of hard
light.

She had so little to do with him these days it ought to have been easy enough to put him out of her mind. Yet it was strange how she sensed, one day, that all was not as it should be in the McCord scheme of things. She supposed subconciously she had begun to take note of his moment of arrival at the rink and the hour of his departure. Whether it was through the day or in the evening, she had to admit she had grown practised in piecing together the pattern of his coming and going, and knew to a moment now when he would show up.

It was certainly no concern of hers when he failed to put in an appearance at all for three whole sessions. And when there was nothing to be seen of him, if only in an ostensibly distant fashion, the next day, she cynically put it down to excess of work. His various freezing concessions around the town were all-demanding, she knew, as well as the mountain of paper-work which had to be presided over from time to time in the office premises integrated in his desert house.

Just the same, the ache of something not right about the days wouldn't be stilled in her, and one afternoon, using a broken piston on the skate grinder as a reason for visiting the compressor room, she looked around for the familiar big frame, the sight of which could somehow jerk at her heart strings.

But there was only Aziz, the trained technician in attendance. 'But I must see McCord,' Celia insisted, after being fobbed off with the usual reply that the boss was not available. 'The skate grinder is a very important piece of equipment. We've got to have some kind of guidance as to ways of getting it fixed.'

The technician considered. 'I should ring up a local engineering shop. It might be quicker than trying to get in touch with the boss.'

'Quicker?' Celia was both puzzled and impatient. 'What do you mean by that? I could ring him myself if I had his number.'

'Not this number,' Aziz smiled. 'Haven't you heard? Mr McCord has gone to Cairo. I'm sorry, but I have no idea when he'll be back.'

'Cairo!' Celia realised she must have sounded shocked, so quickly she tempered her exclamation with a weakly smiling, 'Ah well, I expect the engineering shop will be best,' and left.

But how she got back across the street she never recalled. Cairo! Cairo! Wasn't that where Mandy Bennet had been working all these weeks? Blind to all but her own thoughts, she found herself back in the rink; a rink that no longer had the reassuring, if annoying, feel of McCord's presence in the background.

Why had he gone to Cairo? As if she didn't know. She blinked back a brightness in her eyes. It was crazy to feel this shattered just because her boss had decided to renew his love life. But she did.

Not even Tariq with his increasing attentiveness could help her to surmount the blackest period of her life, though of course she gave no indication outwardly that all was not as it should be.

She went about her business at the ice rink with a serenity that might have been in danger of cracking if it hadn't been for Tariq's nearness. He was extremely handsome and likeable, she told herself, whereas McCord was craggy, overbearing, arrogant—and she missed him!

But all things pass, or so Celia hoped. Moving close to Tariq in the subdued lighting of some modern discotheque or viewing the moonlit waters of the Gulf with him, she was at last living her own life. And at least McCord would have approved of that, wouldn't he?

She had stopped counting the days of the ice rink's drifting without that certain central force, like a ship without a helmsman; though she, like the rest of McCord's underlings, were well trained by now, Celia conjectured wryly. They all functioned like clockwork with or without his vital presence. And it was like him to reappear after several days' absence, unannounced as usual, as though to bask in the knowledge that he had a well-oiled staff.

He blew in—Celia could think of no better way to sum up his entry—one evening when she was standing with Tariq in the fairly crowded coffee lounge. There was still a good half of the session to go, but as always at this late hour no one had any use for her talents as an instructress, so she was spending the time until they closed, as she often did, in Tariq's company.

He greeted his friend effusively. 'McCord! When did you get back?'

'A short while ago.' A tight grin accompanied the reply. Only minutes by the look of it, Celia thought. He looked travel-weary, or was that a deep-down weariness in his eyes? There was no knowing, for the light in them when he glanced her way was challengingly intense as always.

Her own gaze, she hoped, showed none of the lack-lustre detachment it had acquired during his absence. If it was mildly aglow now it was, of course, because she found Tariq's chat so amusing.

'How was Cairo?' he asked, ordering another coffee at the bar. So Tariq knew about McCord's visit to the Egyptian capital. He probably knew also, as the two men were in each other's confidence, that Mandy Bennet was the reason for the trip.

'Great as always,' she heard McCord replying easily. 'The Midan el Tahir—or should I say Liberation Square—right beside the Nile, was a sight for sore eyes. I had trouble with a hotel booking and had to transfer to the Nile Hilton, but the view more than made up for the misunderstanding . . .'

Afraid that he was going to get too poetic about his activities, Celia cut in, 'Do you know Cairo, Tariq?'

'But yes,' he smiled, showing his pearly teeth. 'We have shipping offices in the city. Also I have numerous relatives on the east bank. My mother is of Egyptian

blood, so our family ties with the country are extensive.'
He put an arm round her waist and added, 'You must
make the trip with me some time, and meet my Egyptian
cousins.'

'I'd like to very much, Tariq,' Celia said for McCord's
benefit. He might have spiked her last proposed trip
abroad with Tariq, and that was a hint to say that he was
not likely to be successful a second time. Her smile said
as much. It was scorched momentarily by McCord's
flame-throwing, if lazy, blue glance, but there was
nothing in his smile to give her the satisfaction she had
hoped for in making the remark.

In fact there was nothing at all about him that would
give her a clue as to what he had been up to in Cairo. It
was galling to have to admit that she was eaten up with
curiosity. Why had he made a visit to Cairo at such
short notice? To see Mandy? Well, obviously. But was a
few days of her company sufficient to console him
against her continued absence in Bahrain? How Celia
ached to know. And how difficult it was to have to put
on an indifferent front when McCord was so aggravatingly noncommittal about it all.

She wished now she hadn't stopped him at the beginning, but knowing him he had probably had no intention of giving them more than a descriptive account
of the seasonal splendours of the city, as he was doing
now.

He left before the rink closed, to catch up on some
much-needed sleep, Celia suspected. Or to withdraw to
his desert domain with his recent memories of being
alone with Mandy in an exciting capital like Cairo. The
thought ruined the rest of the evening for Celia, but she
was careful not to spoil things for Tariq, and gave not a
hint in her manner that dinner together at the Holiday
Inn night club was not the best one she had ever had.

She was keyed up all the next day, knowing that the
businesslike McCord would have to call in sooner or

later to check on the backlog of order and delivery slips
that had built up in the ice-rink office. Though she told
herself she was well prepared for his visit, his arrival
when she was just preparing for the opening of the
evening session set her nerves twanging, and made a
knot of the suppressed emotion in her stomach.

His coming made not the slightest difference to her
changing routine, for she only had to replace her shoes
with ice skates. While McCord leafed casually through
the chits, signing one here and there where it was necessary, she busied herself at her locker, making a great show
of ignoring him.

But perhaps her fingers trembled slightly at the
charged atmosphere which always blew up like a sandstorm whenever they were together in the office, for the
pearls she was privately transferring from her handbag
to a hidden cavity in the locker suddenly slithered
from her grasp and went clattering across the tiled
floor.

Of course McCord would have to get there first, and
retrieving them he hung on to them annoyingly with a
musing, 'Well, well, well!' as he examined them.
Obviously aware of their value, he looked sharply quizzical as he looked at her. 'You're taking a chance, aren't
you,' he said,' leaving your expensive tokens around in
a populated place like the ice rink?'

'They're a gift from Tariq,' Celia felt impelled to
labour the point carelessly.

'Of course, the pearl fisher himself.'

Did he *have* to refer to their romantic interlude on
the blue Gulf waters?

'He absolutely insists that I wear them for our dates
after work,' she shrugged, 'so what can I do?'

McCord had moved nearer. She didn't think he
looked refreshed after his break from business. If anything he appeared more drawn, or was it his taut smile
as he spoke which gave this effect? 'Any more priceless
acquisitions I suggest you give to me to put in the office

safe. We're likely to have a stampede if you go on hawking them around like everyday trinkets.'

'I'll think about it.' Celia put on a considering look. 'I do think there's a certain taint attached, don't you, to locking away one's personal possess——'

She got no further in her blithe small talk, for McCord had grabbed her to him with a force reminiscent of that night on the deck of the *Sea Roc*, and in menacing tones he bit out, 'You little idiot! When are you going to learn that you're playing with fire, and in the end it's going to be more than those lovely eyelashes of yours that are going to get singed?'

Her heart raced, close to him once again, her whole being rejoiced in his nearness, while her mind supplied her with the cool reply, 'Aren't you over-dramatising things somewhat? I thought Tariq was your friend?'

'He's one of the best I've got, but he's an Arab, a Bedouin, and their ways are not our ways.'

'Our ways!' Celia lifted a disparaging eyebrow. 'You have your ways, McCord, and I have mine. And by the way, how was Mandy when you called on her in Cairo?'

'Very well, as far as I know.'

As far as he *knew*! What kind of a reply was that? Niggled, she felt the need to ascertain, 'You did drop everything and catch a plane, just to go and talk with her, didn't you?'

'That's right, I did.' Everything in her prayed that she had got it wrong somewhere. But McCord's smiling reply, plus the breeziness with which he backed it up, left her with nothing but her superior confidence where Tariq was concerned. As she defiantly put all this into her attitude, locked as she was in McCord's arms, and he arrogantly made it clear that Mandy was uppermost in *his* mind, the sandstorm was in danger of becoming laced with sheet lightning.

But as it happened the only flashes were the flickering of neon lights beyond the office as staff, opening the rink to the public, went round pressing switches. On view from outside now, McCord quickly let Celia go, and trembling more than she cared to show, she turned at once to the task of donning her skate-boots.

If she could have got them on in record time, nothing would have pleased her more than to make a haughty exit leaving McCord to it in the office. But her limbs were weak, and there were more surprises in store.

She had only just got the right boot laced up when she sensed some kind of commotion in the office door-way. Head bent over her task, that was the only way she could describe it, a sort of excited rustling of air, a quivering, laughing force that compelled her to raise her head just as the whirlwind was gusting in.

'Hi, folks, I made it! I skated all the way! No, don't believe that. How could I with these pesky deserts out-side every town? Gee, the heat! But oh, the Bahrainis! Can I come in?'

Celia raised herself, riveted at the altogether stage entrance of the girl whose likeness hung on the wall. She would never have believed it possible, but the lovely picture that had tormented her all these weeks was actually insipid compared to the real thing.

Mandy Bennet was five foot something of mercurial womanhood, with laughing hazel eyes and thick, tumbl-ing wavy hair of gleaming copper which on anyone else would have looked slinky, but the fresh almost coun-trified features toned it down to just plain beauty. She had a figure, clothed at the moment in hip-hugging jeans and frilly top, that no woman should be obliged to con-template, and a wholly unfeline air that evoked admira-tion rather than envy.

The shutter of Celia's mind had taken this in, in a fraction of a second, for there was no pausing for breath with this effervescent creature, as she was to find, and in the next one she had hurtled into the room straight into McCord's arms, the attractive American drawl all over him. 'Kent! Garsh, it's good to see you! I got your message and came as soon as I could.'

Kent! Celia viewed McCord with studied irony where he was almost lost in the tumbling tresses. So he did have something as lowly and purely mortal as a Christian name after all! His answering immodest glint held hers momentarily, then Mandy was turning in his arms like a tawny tornado to explain, 'Heck, I'm sorry I wasn't in Cairo when you came. We'd just started off on a local tour ... but I expect they told you that at the digs. I was in El Faiyum, as a matter of fact. You know, the sheikhs are crazy to see us flip around on the ice. But if you have to do a solo stint in some official gathering they expect you to make like a tent on skates in the regulation caftan. Can you imagine!'

Her laughter was light as candyfloss which could quickly melt to self-reproach, and with her curving red lips smooching against McCord's cheek, she was, in the next breath, all apology. 'What hellish luck, you coming all the way to Cairo to see me. Was it too awful, honey?'

'As a matter of fact, no,' McCord grinned after he had held her close for long enough, heaven knew, Celia thought. 'I managed to fill in the time in a professional capacity. There's no shortage of work as an ice-engineer in a city like Cairo.'

Of course not, and how typically McCord-like to fit business in somewhere. His love life had suffered a temporary setback with Mandy missing from the scene, but he had made good use of the time, and she was here now, obviously as keen to be with him as he was to be with her.

Celia bolstered her plummeting spirits with bright thoughts of her own Arab boy-friend. Well, they would make a striking foursome—Mandy and McCord, and herself and Tariq.

'Oh, what a tactless screwy I am!' Celia realised that this bubbling contrition was for her ears. 'Please forgive me for hogging McCord like this. I'm always forgetting my manners.'

'This is Celia Darwell, who took over the job you were going to do,' McCord made the introductions. 'Miss Darwell, meet Amanda Bennet of world-wide skating fame.'

'Ignore the showbiz plug,' the coppery radiance said with a merry gleam. 'And McCord knows I'm Mandy to all my friends.'

Celia had expected a formal handshake, but discovered instead her cheek brushing the other girl's as she was given a friendly hug. Her warmth was catching and Celia found herself saying, and meaning it, 'Welcome to the Alhambra, Mandy. I hope you'll have many happy skating days here.'

'That all depends on what the big boss has got lined up for me.'

A conspiratorial twinkle accompanying this remark was not lost on McCord, and unhesitatingly he replied, 'There's enough work here to keep two ice instructresses going. You'll be able to take some of the pressure off Miss Darwell, Mandy. She's been feeling the pace lately . . . what with one thing and another.'

There was no mistaking the hidden meaning in the tail end of his comment. Not to Celia, at least. She knew he was referring to Tariq, and her spirited glance momentarily tying with his told him what she was always at pains to point out. That he might own her working time, but he didn't own her!

However, deep down inside her there was another kind of commotion going on. Mandy's finally turning up for her role at the rink could have had other repercussions. Celia could have found herself out of a job. Was there really enough work for both her and Mandy? she wondered. What doubts she had were dispelled by the easing of some inner tension. McCord seemed to think so, and after all, he was running things.

He was saying now, 'I'll leave it to the two of you to work out your duty programme. No doubt you'll have your own ideas of how you want to run things between yourselves.'

Mandy shrugged. 'Celia knows the ropes. I'll fall in with her way easy enough, I guess. I don't have any plans for messing up what's probably a settled routine.'

'But, Mandy!' Celia was amazed. 'You've had masses more experience than I have. Of course you must take charge now.'

The other girl laughed and linked her arm in McCord's. 'We're all in this together, honey. And I reckon we'll make out as a team. What do you say, boss?'

McCord's reply was to untwine his linked arm and put it squeezingly round the ice star's shoulders. 'Sounds fine to me,' he smiled. 'In any case, it's good to have you here at last, Mandy.'

Celia had to stand by and watch this demonstration of affection. And if she was left in any doubt as to his satisfaction in having Mandy with him, here in Bahrain, McCord's blue glint directed across the top of the tawny tresses her way clinched it.

CHAPTER ELEVEN

Two pairs of feet instead of one certainly made things smoother at the Alhambra ice-rink. Mandy Bennet was beautiful, talented and utterly likeable; a combination practically unknown among the female species, and especially in the show business field. Celia felt decidedly drab by the side of her mercurial charm. Not that she was given any reason to, for Mandy played down all her advantages.

She was quite content to dress in conservative slacks and top for her job as skating coach, as Celia did. And though she obviously possessed tremendous skill on the ice, she did her work-outs privately before the public were allowed in, and without any fuss.

But Celia was not entirely in agreement with this dousing down of one's natural talents. She had practically got a show organised with the help of her star pupils, and it struck her that Mandy would be magnificent in the leading role.

She put it to her one afternoon when trade was slack and they were each enjoying a soft drink at the bar. Mandy pondered, having heard Celia's description of the show so far. 'You mean you want me to flip around a bit in some spangled, feathery get-up?'

'Oh, have you got something like that?' Celia pounced on the idea enthusiastically. 'It would be just the thing to give our small effort some professional glamour.'

'Well, I brought a few show dresses with me. I reckon I can deck out in ostrich feathers and sequins and do one of my solo routines, if you're sure you don't mind?'

'Mind?' Celia echoed smilingly. 'They're going to be tumbling over themselves at the door to get a look at the world-famous Mandy Bennet! And that will be wonderful for the children's morale.'

'Okay, consider me roped in,' Mandy said with good-humoured resignation. 'When is it to be, this world premiere of ours?'

'In two weeks' time on a Saturday night. The children are having their costumes made for the performance, and as I'm learning,' Celia said with a wry grin,' nothing moves with any great speed out here.'

With the work shared nowadays there was often time for a chat, and on another occasion Mandy started off, a little out of character for her, in a subdued way, 'You've met my father, I believe?'

Celia nodded, not knowing quite how to frame an answer. 'I like him a lot,' she smiled. 'You remind me of him in many ways, Mandy . . . although I can't say our meeting gave me much opportunity to——'

'Yes, I know,' the other girl cut her off. 'He . . . he wasn't himself. McCord told me all about that day when the two of you had to take Dad home, and how you helped to get him . . . on his feet again for an important oilfield pow-wow . . . I've been wanting to thank you for some time . . .'

'I was just glad to be of some use. It was nothing really . . .' Celia's throat grew pink. What she had done for Mike had long since slipped her mind, but apparently it hadn't McCord's.

Mandy's subdued gaze had grown distant. 'It's been bad for Dad. Since Mom died he seems to have lost the spark for making a life for himself. I've had my work, friends, the discipline of performing before an audience. It hasn't been easy, but I've gotten over the worst. With Dad it's different. He married Mom when she was just eighteen, and from the start she went with him on every oil assignment. Their travels to every part of the world were just one long honeymoon.' Mandy gave a lopsided smile. 'They didn't even decide to have me until their marriage was fifteen years old.' And then heavily again, 'Mom fell sick almost overnight. She'd lived and thrived

in some of the lousiest spots on this earth. She was as
strong as a donkey—or so we all thought—but pneu-
monia's a strange malady. She died within a few hours
of being laid low.'

There was a silence when Mandy had finished. Celia
could think of no words of consolation. Nor did she
feel that Mandy needed them now. It was Mike,
Mandy's father, who had to be shown that a partnership
could continue, even if one could only go along beside
the other in spirit.

McCord seldom came to the ice rink office these days.
That he was busy with his deep-freeze plants and refrigerating schemes and deliveries of iced foodstuffs for
the Sheikh's banquets Celia didn't doubt. But his evenings were reserved for Mandy, that much she knew.

Dining with Tariq in the upstairs Alhambra restaurant, she was discovering, was not only being in a
position to be seen from the shadowy areas of the closed
rink, but also to see. And many were the nights when
her digestion was upset at the sight of McCord and
Mandy talking earnestly in the dimly-lit office below, or
leaving together with McCord's protective arm around
the other girl as they disappeared towards the outdoors.

Celia didn't know why she should let herself feel so
miserable on these occasions. After all, she knew the
score where the two of them were concerned. McCord
had flown to Cairo to tell Mandy that he wanted her
close to him in Bahrain. And would Mandy have turned
her back on fame and fortune as a world star for a
lowly job as ice-instructress, if she wasn't in full agreement with this?

Celia made every effort to dull her awareness of
Mandy's and McCord's togetherness by losing herself
doggedly in Tariq's company. She was really extremely
fond of her Arab escort and he gave every indication of
being devoted to her. Of course, by now she had been in
his arms often, under the Gulf moon on midnight strolls,
and in the shadows of the rink's car park, if they were

going their different ways after the evening session. But never once had she been able to stop herself comparing Tariq's kiss with that of McCord's that night on the deck of the *Sea Roc*.

One was like the pleasant caress of the sea's ripple on an acquiescent shore; the other a crashing, earth-moving force that pounded the rocks of her defences demanding not only acquiescence but all-out and uncompromising surrender. And it wasn't just the anger of the moment, or the impatience in that embrace on the starlit deck. It was something else; something that would always be there waiting to be sparked off in the same way. And she despaired of knowing it in any other man.

The days at the ice-rink were growing busier, with more people, mainly the European contingent, trying out their skills on the ice. But the evenings were inclined to be social affairs when the Alhambra was used mostly as a meeting place. This allowed for lots of free time for drifting around the coffee lounge.

Tariq had many friends among the Bahraini patrons and Celia often chatted alongside him. Some nights Mandy and McCord joined them. For Celia these were the more trying occasions. She was impressed by Tariq's loyalty to her, when there were delectable, effervescent redheads around like the American ice-star. In fact it helped her to ride McCord's, as always, unappreciative smile whenever her glance ran up against his.

Mandy joked with Tariq and he with her, but it was in a frothy way with no depth and they both knew it was simply a device for passing the time. In any case, Celia reminded herself, as they were good friends each man would obviously respect the other's property.

Celia made a wry face to herself at the thought of being owned by any man, yet she was not without a certain awareness that she was sailing dangerously close to becoming Tariq's exclusive possession.

Just how close was brought home to her one sunny

afternoon when she had left her suite at the hotel, after the lunch break, to start out for work. Not only was it a surprise to find Tariq waiting for her in the lobby, it was also a puzzlement, for he invariably spent long hours in his office and had little time for social calls through the day.

'Tariq!' She voiced her thoughts with the laughing exclamation. 'What on earth are you doing here at this hour of the day?'

'I wanted to see you for something very special.' He kissed her fondly and for Celia a little embarrassingly among the coming and going of the hotel guests. Then taking her hand he said blithely, 'Come. You will see that I have left my desk for an excellent reason.'

The mystery deepening, Celia went with him to the outdoors. They bypassed her car outside the hotel, and his own parked next to it, and she tilted an eyebrow wonderingly. Tariq never went anywhere on foot . . .

She was conscious of the minutes ticking by. She had already left herself scant time to get to the rink before opening time. And though she would not have wanted to spoil Tariq's obvious pleasure in what he was about she did have to stifle a mounting irritation at these wasted moments.

They stopped on the corner of the hotel block at last. There was little traffic here. What now? She resisted the desire to take a look at her watch, and saw Tariq snap his fingers in the autocratic way of the well-bred Arab. The next moment a gleaming silver shape was put into motion under a hotel parking archway and with the whispering of its expensive inner parts slid to a stop right beside them.

Celia forced a smile. 'I'm sorry, Tariq, I really can't go anywhere with you now . . . I'm already late for——'

'*I'm* not going anywhere, my dear,' Tariq smiled. 'You are. This will be your mode of transport from now on in Bahrain.'

Celia was dumbstruck. She stared at the Lamborghini,

a silver dream of a car, priceless in its field, with every known luxury attachment incorporated in its low, wide, streamlined magnificence, and dreamlike herself, she exclaimed, 'Tariq! I couldn't drive round town in this!'

'Why not? I do in mine,' Tariq laughed. 'And how do you propose to get to your work, my love?' With this his glance had moved playfully along the street to where his chauffeur, who had unknown to her left the Lamborghini, as though obeying orders, was now climbing into her car. The next moment she saw it move away and disappear along the street into the busy stream of traffic.

'Oh no!' She looked at her watch. 'Now what am I going to do?'

'You have but one choice, darling,' Tariq twinkled. He opened the door of the Lamborghini with a flourish and a trace of that insistence that had accompanied his presenting her with the expensive pearl necklace. 'I wish you to accept this little gift, not only because for you to do so would mean a great deal to me, but also as an Al Rahma I cannot have someone who is close to my heart driving around in a nondescript vehicle of a type used by the lower classes in the town.'

Celia wanted to ask why not? But she had no time to waste in arguing. Mandy would not cope on her own now with the somewhat rougher types who were frequenting the ice rink in the afternoons. As though reading her thoughts Tariq said, 'Your car has gone to join its workmates in McCord's garages. This now is for your comfort and my family's prestige. Accept it with my love and I will be the happiest man in the world.'

Celia felt that prestige and love had a way of becoming confused here, but it was not something she could put into words. Nor could she think of a thing to say in response to the stunning realisation that Tariq calmly expected her to take over some thirty thousand pounds' worth of glittering car, and regard it as her own. She could only smile and say, 'We'll talk about it later, Tariq.'

She might have known that whatever she said he would regard as an acceptance, for smiling too as he helped her into the car, he said obliquely, 'We will meet tonight as usual ... and you may thank me any way you wish.'

He closed the door and gave her a wave before hurrying back to his own jade and chrome palace on wheels. Celia had gathered earlier on in their relationship that Tariq belonged to a wealthy family, but this, she told herself, eyeing the leopard-skin covered seats of her own interior, the walnut and gold panelled dashboard, was ridiculous!

She was treated to another gay wave as Tariq slid away from the kerb, and then flicking the keys of her own machine, not without a certain amusement at the sly way Tariq had left her without a leg—or a wheel in this case—to stand on, she gave a sigh of resignation and set off for work.

Actually the Lamborghini she was driving attracted no special attention on her way to the ice-rink. Practically every well-to-do family owned some such status symbol of wealth in oil-rich Bahrain, and the streets were more inclined to be cluttered with these high-powered jewels of the road than the lowly run-abouts, similar to her usual form of transport.

As for speed, her present steed certainly got her to work in record time, but parking on this and successive occasions proved difficult.

Of course Celia had known from the start that she couldn't accept the Lamborghini as a permanent gift. But she was aware also that she would have to use caution when returning it to Tariq. He could, as she had seen, be somewhat rigorous in his desires, and it might soften the blow if she waited until she found a way to reclaim her company car.

In the meantime finding a place for the Lamborghini in the small space allocated for staff parking behind the rink, was proving a headache. It was not only that it

took up more than twice the space of her other car. It
also had the embarrassing effect of standing out with a
kind of obscene opulence when ranged alongside the
modest and sometimes decrepit runabouts of the rink
employees. She had often gone indoors feeling uneasy
about its ostentatiousness. But as it was too long to park
in the street there was nothing to be done but edge the
Lamborghini in somewhere each time she came to work,
even if it did appear to take up all the space and more
available.

Of course it would have to be at its most awkward
angle one night when McCord drove up just as she was
leaving.

Tariq had had to miss the evening session because of a
dinner with business associates and Celia was looking
forward to a pleasant soak in the bath in her suite at the
hotel and an early night. Mandy was still indoors and
Celia would have preferred to make a quick getaway
before McCord's arrival to pick her up. She and
McCord seldom had a word for each other these days,
and to have to witness his devotion to the other girl,
fond as she was herself of Mandy, was something that
Celia had no stomach for.

But luck would have it that she was just making for
the Lamborghini when McCord swung in and found his
way barred. But of course that didn't stop McCord. He
manoeuvred a passage for himself despite the scant
lighting at the rear of the building and, paintwork
almost mingling with paintwork, brought his own car to
a stop in its usual haunt.

Celia heard the door slam and across the gleaming
width of the Lamborghini bonnet, the bulk of McCord
appeared almost with a leisurely air. But there was a
hard light in his eyes and a twist about his smile in the
shadows as he spoke. 'It would be a great help,' he said,
'if you would keep your expensive trinkets from under
other people's feet. This, as you may have noticed, is a

parking lot, not a display area for your romantic acquisitions.'

The harsh sarcasm in his tones brought the colour to Celia's cheeks. 'It happens to be the form of transport I prefer,' she lied. 'And as I'm only a simple employee here, I've no choice but to put my "trinket" in the space provided.'

'It would be more at home, I'm sure, in the patrons' parking area. There's bound to be at least one other trendy example of Arab over-indulgence with which it would make a cosy twosome.'

Celia knew that in his satirical way he was referring to Tariq's car, and as subtly as she could manage she replied, 'Obviously it's more suited to the roominess there. If you have no objections . . .'

'None at all,' said McCord before moving indoors. 'It will be nice not to have to clamber over the oversized token of a tender relationship every time one wants to get in the rink.'

Left alone in the darkness, Celia closed her eyes over her choking resentment. That did it! She hadn't wanted the Lamborghini. She hated its ostentatious opulence, but she would drive it now. Oh yes! For as long as she stayed in Bahrain at least she would consider it her personal property. And she would continue to leave it in the employees' parking space. There was room for both hers *and* McCord's, as he had demonstrated, and gritting her teeth as she extricated herself from the predicament he had left her in, she sailed away without a scratch on either vehicle to prove it.

And she went on proving it in the days ahead. Tariq was delighted to see her using his gift to her with such gay abandon, so at least someone was pleased, Celia mused sourly.

How far her defiance of McCord's advice was taking her, she had no time to worry over, for all was now constant activity at the ice-rink in preparation for the ice carnival.

Mandy had done most of the organising. For a start she knew all about show business, but more important than this was the fact that she had only to make some request to McCord either for extra seating round the ice, or colourful spotlights to be mounted, and the thing was done.

Celia had decided to take no part in the show herself. She wanted to be on hand to give encouragement to the children behind the scenes, and though Mandy was reluctant to occupy the limelight, she had to agree that Celia would be needed backstage.

On the night of the performance there was an atmosphere of pleasurable anticipation in the interior of the rink. Coloured lights lit the expanse of ice that would be 'the stage', and friends and relatives of the Arab children, those who were not tied by family traditions which would prevent them from attending such a function, filled the extra rows of seats around the edge.

When the music started for the opening of the display Celia found she was more jittery than any of the children. Eleven-year-old Ahmad was the first out into the spotlights, and she saw at once through a gap in the back curtains that her choice had been right. Ahmad was always supremely confident on the ice, and tonight with members of his family present he demonstrated his abilities to whizz around on blades with verve and polish. Perhaps he put a little bit too much drama in his actions when interpreting his choice of music, but this only delighted the audience and brought him a terrific burst of applause when he was completing his final spin.

The other children were inspired by the sound. Eager as they were to show off too, and with none of the inhibitions and shyness known by children of a more sophisticated society, it became a contest to see who would induce the most enchanted reaction from the people in the seats.

Of course there were disasters. Seven-year-old Husain,

a little too keen, got his skates entangled at the start, and slid out into the centre of the ice on his bottom. But with childlike unconcern he picked himself up and went on to do his spot as though all entrances were made this way. Pretty Latifa had a fall during her interpretation of The Swan. She came back behind the curtain to recover, then went out to execute a charming performance for one so small.

Yes, sometimes with a little dampness in her eyes when she peeped out through the curtains, Celia felt she had just cause to be proud. All her pupils were showing that her coaching had proved worth it, and that for any teacher was the finest reward.

In the glow beyond the ice she could make out the faces of the audience. Many of the Bahrainis she knew quite well by now, especially the *ayahs* of the children who were out in force to beam on the marvels of their own individual charges.

McCord was there, standing offside, a little aloof, as befitting the boss of the place. He had entered into the spirit of the thing by wearing evening dress. Celia felt an odd catch at her heart at the sight of him, making everyone else in the place appear so insignificant, or so it seemed to her, with his vital presence.

She had just cause to thank him for providing unstintingly everything that had been needed to give a show atmosphere at the rink; although, she reminded herself, Mandy had done all the asking, not her. And it was for Mandy, she was certain, that everything had been done to ensure the show's success.

The other girl was kept busy doing pantomime bits which allowed for the children to be on the ice all at the same time. The two of them had worked this out as a way of breaking the monotony of continuous solo performances, and the idea was proving a success. Mandy was wonderful as the Pied Piper with all the little tailed marvels on ice following her make-believe flute. And in a mock desert encampment with stuffed toy camels in reclining pose and sleeping mats and cooking pots over red glows, to give the effect of night time, the ice-star was magical as a midnight marauder.

But the highlight of the show was to be Mandy in her solo spot for the finale. When the time came the atmosphere in the rink was tense with expectation. The children, having enjoyed tumultuous applause for their efforts, went to sit with their families on the rink's perimeter. And with no duties for the moment to keep her behind the scenes, Celia, in a dress of dove-grey watered silk, tiny diamanté stars in her ears giving her a poised look, joined Tariq who had just recently arrived.

Unfortunately he had chosen to pass the time between the scenes by chatting to his friend the rink boss. Celia would have preferred to be anywhere but right next to McCord at this moment, considering what was about to take place. But when the music started and the lights dropped low she concentrated on the expanse of ice.

Mandy appeared like a golden vision in the spotlight and had the audience transfixed from the moment she struck off at speed. In saffron ostrich feathers and sequinned primrose tunic, shapely legs unadorned for freedom of movement, she was truly a queen on blades. Though she made no great effort to overshadow the previous performances of keen young amateurs her very presence on the ice was bewitching, riveting all who watched her.

She had chosen music lilting, but with fire, and the more difficult her programme appeared the more she seemed to float smilingly through the tremendous leaps and splits and whirling contortions that made her a world name. Moved at the girl's tremendous skill, Celia obeyed an impulse to slant her gaze sideways. The stark appeciation displayed on McCord's face as he watched the beautiful nymph-like figure speeding like the wind over the glossy surface was not entirely unexpected, though for Celia it was like a knife-thrust in her heart.

At the last goddess-like leap and fountain-flow of a spin, she clapped as loud as the rest, but that look she had seen on McCord's face would, she felt, remain forever engraved on her heart.

Tariq, his arm about her waist in the commotion of the lights going up and people preparing to leave, was keen too to make for somewhere where he could have her to himself, now that all the fuss was over. But Celia's work was far from finished. 'I can't go yet, Tariq,' she explained smilingly. 'The children will need help with their dressing, and I'll have to see that there's no mix-up with the costumes that they'll want to take with them. You can wait if you like, but I don't expect I'll be through until late.'

Tariq shrugged and kissed her there and then under the bright lights. 'I am very jealous of these young performers who take up so much of your time,' he flashed her a half-laughing look. 'But as tomorrow is Sunday and we can spend the whole day together, I will allow myself to be upstaged this time.'

Celia hurried off towards the area behind the curtains, more as a means of escaping McCord's all-pervading presence than with any great enthusiasm for work. She found the American girl trying to establish order in what sufficed as a dressing room. 'Mandy, you were terrific!' Celia went to embrace her.

'Thanks.' Always modest, Mandy put on a dry look. 'I guess I dazzled the audience a bit, but I think the kids stole my thunder.'

She helped for a while in righting things behind the scenes, but then Celia sent her on her way. It had been a strenuous evening for Mandy with her numerous appearances on the ice, whereas she, Celia, had been just a general factotum behind the glamour, and it was up to her now to clear away where it was necessary.

It was after midnight before she had satisfied herself that all was in order apart from the dismantling of the back curtains which the workmen would attend to another day. The rink was totally deserted by this time and sunk in the gloom of disuse. She made her way out into the night with mixed feelings. Part of her was happy at what the children had achieved this evening, but outweighing this was an acute feeling of dispiritedness.

She was rooting for her car keys in her handbag beside the Lamborghini when a voice from the interior said, 'The door's open.'

Celia peered in, startled. McCord! When she had recovered herself she said with annoyance and distrust, 'You've been rifling my locker in the office.'

'That's right. I took the liberty of filching your keys. As you've been working with such devotion for the good of the rink, I thought the least I could do was chauffeur you home.'

She didn't know what to make of his tones. She thought she sensed menace there, certainly sarcasm and a kind of steely self-restraint. But she was tired and in no mood to pit herself emotionally against his granite charm.

She dropped into her seat, and as he closed the door across her there was a look on his face which she found vaguely disturbing. But was there ever a time, she asked herself wearily, when McCord wasn't disturbing?

She left it to him to see her back to the hotel. The first inclination she had that he had never had any intention of driving her straight there came almost in the first moments, for he thundered away with unnecessary speed from the parking lot. Then before she knew it they were hurtling towards the highway out of town.

So their few moments together were destined, as always, to be explosive, and she draped back with resignation. She had no fear with McCord at the controls, but when they were approaching more than a hundred miles an hour on the deserted highway she was sufficiently angered to remark, 'It's a little late, don't you think, for games? Some of us have had a long day.'

'And a long night too ... some of us,' came the drawling reply. Celia couldn't make out what he meant by that, unless he was hinting, as usual, at the time she had spent with Tariq, during working hours. 'And what better way to round off such a great evening,' he went on with a grim smile, pushing up the speedometer, 'than to see just what this oversized token of friendship we're travelling in is capable of on the road. Don't you agree?'

'I know that I'm tired,' she said flatly, ignoring his mood and the alarming speed they were doing. 'And I would like to turn in before the dawn hours if that's possible.'

'Oh, you'll be doing that.' There was something distinctly ominous about his grin. 'In fact you should be all tucked up, I'd say, within the next half hour.'

Whatever it was that had driven him to race the Lamborghini almost to its limits through the night seemed to peter out, for with no less dark-faced intensity he slackened down to a more breatheable speed after a while.

It was then that Celia saw where they were heading and, stiffening, she said, 'Unless you're planning to make the return trip in the same crazy fashion you're going to be hard put to it to get me back to the Gulf Hotel in the time stated.'

McCord said nothing for a moment. His face seemed carved out of teak in the shadows. Only his narrowed eyes and his smile gave any indication of thought or feeling—and what they were was anybody's guess.

Just when Celia thought no answer would be forthcoming he put in, 'I forgot to mention, you won't be staying at the Gulf Hotel any more.'

The apprehension that had been building up in her all evening she had put down to the strain of having to nurse the show through to its final stages without any major disasters. Now she knew that that had been child's play compared to what she was going through at this moment.

Forcing herself to speak evenly, she said, 'If this is another way of telling me I've got the sack, aren't you being rather elaborate about your choice of setting?'

'Who said anything about the sack?' He steered with a casual air. 'We don't work that way in Bahrain. If you remember, I agreed to employ you so that you could remain on the island. The papers I signed gave me full control of your services for a period of six months. You've worked for me how long? ... four months? ... That means as your employer you still owe me two months of your time.'

The rush of relief in Celia was almost like a pain, though she spoke ironically enough. 'I think I can just about finish my stint at the rink, as I've come this far.'

There was another silence which, to her seemed to build up to nerve-racking proportions, then McCord said, 'That's something else I forgot to mention. I'm closing the rink as from tonight. It's proved a success in a way, but it's not quite my line.'

Celia was shattered by this news. 'The children are going to miss their practice,' was the only comment she could salvage from her devastated thoughts.

'They'll find other outlets for their energies,' McCord shrugged. 'I don't think Bahrain is going to fold up exactly at finding itself without an ice-rink.'

Celia felt numbed. But through the shock of what she had just heard something like an explanation came to her.

Why did it have to be tonight that McCord had decided to close down the rink? For it was a snap decision, she was sure. She gulped quietly. Did she have to ask herself this question when she had seen that look on McCord's face during the show? He had decided that he didn't want to share Mandy, who had been dazzling on the ice, with anyone; least of all, all the other males whose gazes must have been every bit as appreciative as his, if Celia had thought to look around.

It was drastic action, to close down the rink because of a personal possessiveness, but only what one would expect from a man like McCord.

A new kind of resentment flared in her at finding herself without a job or a roof over her head in a matter of minutes and she spoke up quiveringly. 'I suppose it suits you to play the iron-handed boss, once in a while?'

'Annoyed because of all the fun you'll miss?' His smile held a certain sadistic satisfaction.

Celia let him have his little joke, which went a lot deeper, she felt, than she had the clarity of mind to fathom. Besides, they had arrived at El Zommorro and she was curious as to why he had brought her here at this hour of the night—or should she say morning?

There was a hush over the grounds as they alighted from the car. The house, resplendent and white under the glow of a crescent moon, stood amid green stretches, and the perfume of night blossom and roses hung on the air. Celia was reluctant to stir from where she could see the gardens stretching to the edge of the desert. Even McCord's presence had little effect on the spell of witnessing the beauty and the savagery of nature in one setting; perhaps because for all his city dealings he belonged here, was part of these conflicting surroundings. One felt that.

He did finally break the spell by mentioning, 'Much of the greenness was here before the house was built, due to the underground springs. Even the name El Zommorro comes from the old days when it was an oasis. It's a corruption of the word meaning emerald, and somebody must have thought it fitting, surrounded as it is by wilderness.'

Celia was conscious of a strange and abiding peace here. It wasn't the first time she had experienced this sensation and abruptly she cut off any more mind-meandering by asking, 'It may seem a silly question, but where do I fit into your scheme of things, if, as you say, the ice-rink is no longer in existence?'

'I thought you'd gathered.' He took her arm and steered her towards the house. 'As you know, the office side of the business is done mainly here on the premises. It's a thing that's grown with time. In the old days I used to do a lot of the paper work myself, but like all successful businesses it's grown into something of a monster, and soon the whole thing will be transferred to a suitable office block in town. But for now an extra hand on the staff would be useful. No special qualifications are needed.'

They were indoors now, and in the muted glow of the house lights he went on, 'You'll occupy the quarters you used before where you'll find your bags from the hotel have been unpacked. On Monday morning you'll be directed to the office wing and shown your duties.'

Celia digested all this without a word. If she had been about to comment McCord put in, 'Oh, and I should point out that leave from your place of employment is pretty restricted.'

Celia flared then. 'You mean I'm forbidden to leave the house? But that's——'

'I don't think you quite understand how binding a work agreement is in an Arab country,' he cut in smoothly. 'As your employer I have full control of your time.'

'In other words, you've bought me!'

His crooked smile more than a match for her icy satire he left her at the door of her suite with the words, 'You could say that.'

CHAPTER TWELVE

IN the days that followed Celia found herself yet another component in the McCord business set-up, though she couldn't complain of overwork. The office staff, with the exception of Kamel, who kept her at a cool distance as though what had happened between them was entirely her fault, were friendly and helpful. Her rooms were part of the household and she dined downstairs of an evening waited on by Quadi, the softfooted Pakistani servant. But of McCord she saw nothing at all.

With the house and grounds, it seemed, at her disposal she wandered at will. The loveliness and peace of the gardens made her realise how much she had missed the secluded out-of-town life she had been accustomed to in England. Indoors, idling through the cool and beautiful rooms with the masculine touches, the thought that McCord's possessions looked as uncompromising as the man himself brought a wan smile to her lips.

Of course she knew why he wasn't around. He had closed the rink so that he could have Mandy to himself. And by the look of it they were spending every possible moment together. Celia considered she had the whole thing summed up, but then all her surmising was sent awry when Mandy came one afternoon to say goodbye.

'I hope I'm not interrupting work output,' she said mischievously when Celia came to see her after receiving a message in the office.

'Hardly,' Celia smiled leading the way to garden seats on the shady terrace. 'If there is any output I've a feeling I'm not much part of it.'

'I can't stop, honey,' Mandy put out a hand as Celia would have ordered drinks. 'Dad and I are due at the airport in about an hour.'

Celia looked a little stupid. 'Are you leaving Bahrain?'

'Yep, we're going back to the States,' Mandy said happily. 'Dad's been offered a desk job back home—McCord's wangled it, you might know, with the oil chiefs—and we're going to set up house in Beaumont, Texas, not far from his work. It's something I've dreamed of for a long time—the house, I mean, and Dad and I. That's why I hung on in Cairo as long as I could. You need hard cash to buy property, and as I told you, the sheikhs pay well for their entertainment. But then McCord came and told me that Dad was getting deeper into the doldrums . . .'

'You mean,' Celia did her best *not* to look stupid,' McCord came to see you in Cairo to tell you that your father needed you in Bahrain?'

'That was the message I received,' Mandy nodded. 'He told me later that it was you who suggested that I would be more help to Dad here, and you were right. So you see I've got a lot to thank you for. That's why I wanted to do it personally before we left.'

As the other girl gripped her hand warmly Celia said with a sudden pang, 'Then this is goodbye?'

'I'm afraid so,' Mandy grimaced smilingly. 'But we'll keep in touch, and who knows . . . one day . . .'

Celia knew a glimmer of pleasure at the unspoken pact, though hardly listening, she couldn't stop herself from asking, 'But . . . what about McCord?'

'McCord?' Mandy looked blank. 'Well, what about him? He's worked like crazy to get Dad this transfer and he knows I'm grateful, but—Hey, wait a minute!' With a dawning look Mandy chuckled, 'You didn't think that McCord and I . . .?' At Celia's expression she looked doubly amused. 'What, McCord with the computerised emotions? No, he's just a very dear friend of the family.' She became pensive. 'Pop's the only man in my life. We're gonna have a ball setting up house together. I'm gonna train him to put his feet up nights, when he comes home, and try my hand with some of his favourite recipes in the kitchen . . .'

No mention was made of the word sacrifice, but Celia knew. The ice-star was turning her back on fame and success for a worthier cause, and the two girls hugged each other with a choking feeling of affection.

'Goodbye, Mandy!' Some moments later Celia waved her to the car. 'I hope you get everything you've worked for.'

'You too, honey. I'll write.' Mandy threw her a last smile before driving off.

It was some time before Celia could get her mind to function normally again. So it was true what she had thought at the start. The woman who counted first in McCord's life would have to have a powerful attraction to come between him and his work. Mandy, with her freshness and youth and unselfishness, had proved that.

Still she felt a meagre lifting of her spirits as she went indoors. His work was finished now in town. He had done what he could for Mandy's father, which meant that at any moment he would be coming home.

She spent the time listening for his car, and when it arrived, it was silly, she knew, but she went hurrying out on to the drive to greet him. But she had been hasty in assuming that it was McCord's car, for it was Tariq, not he, who stepped out of a chauffeur-driven limousine to meet her.

Perhaps it was her disappointment that gave her the impression that Tariq looked a little sinister in cotton headdress and flowing robe. The kindliness in his eyes had been replaced by a certain annoyance, and when he spoke there was no warm smile to accompany his words. 'It has taken me a week to discover your whereabouts,' he said. 'McCord is never available when you want him and since the rink's closure I haven't had a thing to go on. It was only by insisting on information at the Gulf Hotel that I have managed to trace you here.'

'It's simply a transfer of employment.' Celia tried to

make the comment sound light.

'So I have heard. But that of course is out of the question. As my fiancée you must come with me at once.' He took her arm and began to steer her towards the car.

Gripped by a peculiar apprehension, Celia shook herself free as pleasantly as she could. 'I can't leave, just like that!' she gave a strangled laugh. 'There are certain rules——'

'All of which mean nothing when considering the fact that you belong to me. Now must I be more persuasive, or will you accompany me in a sensible manner to the car?'

Sensible! Celia resisted leaving El Zommorro with everything she possessed. She had a feeling that if she went now it was the end of something imperative in her life. But Tariq called for his chauffeur's assistance and against her will she was bundled into the car and driven away at speed.

When she had recovered her breath she sat up to confront her abductor. 'I don't think this is very funny, Tariq!'

'I am not out to amuse, nor am I myself amused. As you are my future wife your duties towards me should be quite obvious.'

His words annoyed her. 'It's customary to ask a girl first, not just assume that she's ready for marriage,' she said crossly.

'I have been patient,' he shrugged. 'I know the reputation my countrymen have for pushing matters of this nature. I have given you time to familiarise yourself with the idea of being betrothed to an Arab. Now I shall waste no more time. The wedding will take place tonight.'

'Tonight?' In panic Celia argued, 'But, Tariq, you don't understand! I like you . . . I like you a lot . . . but not enough to marry you . . .'

'This has all been decided long ago, my dear. The

gifts I made to you ... the pearls, the powerful car ...
Your acceptance of these things was, in a way, your
acceptance of me as the man who will share your marriage bed.'

'But I never intended to keep the gifts, don't you see?'
Celia was desperate. 'I just did it to get back at McCord.
He was always making out that he owned me, or at
least my time——' She swallowed on this. As it had
turned out, he did! 'I just wanted to let him see that
what I did in my free time was my own business.'

'You should have thought of the consequences earlier,
my dear. Not that it would have made any difference.
My mind was made up from the moment I first saw
you, and the culmination of that dream will be in the
nuptial ceremony in a few hours from now. You will be
dressed as a woman of my country, and later subject
yourself to my will as befitting an Arab wife.'

Celia couldn't believe her ears. It was all so matter-
of-fact. No tenderness now, just clear-cut orders and
instructions. As she eyed Tariq's shrouded profile from
where she was huddled in a corner of the car, it seemed
to her a little hawk-like in the failing light, and she was
reminded of a desert falcon who, having wheeled and
idled long enough, swoops without emotion on his prey.

They had reached Manama and were speeding over the
causeway which led to the adjoining island of Muharraq.
Apart from being aware that this was where many of
the merchant families lived, Celia knew little of this section of Bahrain, and the onion-shaped mosques against
the darkening sky and faded family mansions were as
strange to her as another land.

When they stopped she had scant time to take stock
of her whereabouts, seeing only a magnificent house
built alongside a rambling mud warren which in the old
days must have been the dwelling place for the members
of the Rahma family; then she was hustled indoors to
another warren-like interior, along passages, up winding

staircases and eventually into a room that smelled
strongly of incense.

'Here you will be bathed and dressed for the ceremony.' Tariq was all Arab as he bowed his way backward to the door. His dark eyes lit with passion as he
left her with the words, 'I shall await your company
with eagerness.'

The first thing Celia did was rush round to try all the
doors, but each one was secure and she was a prisoner
in a balconied harem-like interior whose glazed, latticed
doors showed glimpses of a calm, indifferent sea, and
innocently winking stars.

Oh, what a fool she had been, she wailed to herself,
to tamper with the affections of an Arab. But then Tariq
had said he had desired her from the start, so what could
she have done to avoid it?

She paced, determined not to go through with this
crazy wedding, but frighteningly certain that she had no
choice in the matter. It wasn't as though Tariq had
endeared himself to her in this last hour. He was cold
and proud and totally unlike the kindly, gentle person
she had assumed him to be.

She fingered the tinselled robes laid out for her on a
divan and dropped them in panic and distaste. Oh, she
had been warned! Once an Arab, always an Arab, and
a Bedouin at that. Hadn't they once been a nomadic
race? As McCord would have said, Tariq had simply
reverted to nature.

There was the sound of someone at the door and
knowing that at any moment a team of handmaidens
would file in to bathe and anoint her for the nuptial
ceremony, she tensed. But only one person entered the
room—a mature woman with a neat figure in a Paris
afternoon dress and white winged strands at the temples
threaded through the rich dark gloss of a coiffured hair-
do.

As she came forward Celia saw at once the likeness of
Tariq in a face that had a kind of ageless beauty, despite

its faint aura of sadness. 'I am Tariq's mother.' Her smile illuminated all but the shadowed depths of her eyes. 'I have come as a mother should, to welcome her daughter into the family.'

'Mrs ... I mean, Madame Rahma ...' Celia floundered. How did one address an Arab lady? 'I don't want to sound discourteous, but no one has bothered to ask my opinion regarding this marriage.'

Tariq's mother looked concerned, but not surprised. 'My son has always been headstrong,' she said, taking a seat on the divan. 'He tells us nothing of the affairs of his heart, but we are a close family, you understand, and when we are summoned to meet his bride, we assume that she is a willing party to the arrangement.'

Celia said nothing to stress the fact that she had not been consulted, and with a searching sympathy the Arab woman smiled. 'Have you known Tariq long?'

'Oh yes, for several weeks.' Celia's eyes clouded. 'But tonight he's different. I can't believe he's the same charming, kindly man whose company I have often enjoyed.'

'These are the ways of the East, my child.' The sadness in the dark eyes was evident in the smile. 'In our country the wooing ceases at the moment of union and from then on the wife is just the chattel of her husband.'

Celia suppressed a quiet horror at the thought, but she was struck by the way Tariq's mother seemed aware of Western comparison, probably because, as a merchant's wife, she met many Westerners in her daily life.

As they sat together on the divan, the dark eyes had a twinkling scrutiny as they roamed over Celia's smooth features and fair hair. The Arab matron said after a moment, 'I hope you will not be offended if I tell you that I admire my son's taste.'

There was none of the animosity that a mother might feel for a foreign intrusion in her family, but there was no doubt that she was aware of Celia's comparative newness to Bahrain, and with a warmth that was reminiscent of Tariq in the early days the woman asked, 'What brings you to a country so far from home, child?'

Celia smiled forlornly. 'It's a long story. One that I've grown tired of repeating.' She sighed, realising that some explanation was expected. 'You see, it was a crazy idea in the first place. My father was a government official years ago out here. He was going to marry a dancing girl called Nevine, but the wedding was stopped at the last moment and my father was packed off back to England. He married eventually a woman of his own kind, but he was widowed early in life, and from being very young I suppose I've always known that Nevine was the one and only love of my father's life.' Celia let out a breath. 'He died about four months ago and I had this wild urge to know the dancing girl who had meant so much to him, but I've never had any luck in my search for her.'

Without noticing that the woman's features had turned a little waxen she produced the photograph she always carried on her, and shrugged disconsolately. 'No one seems to recall anything surrounding the young government official who was posted here thirty years ago.'

Tariq's mother took the photograph of the smiling fair-haired young man. Her face had gone a strange putty colour under its olive-skinned beauty, and it seemed that the deep well of inner sadness came brimming to the surface in her eyes as a whispered exclamation escaped her lips. 'Peter!'

Celia went rigid where she sat. Never had she heard her father's name spoken in this way before.

As the glistening dark eyes of Tariq's mother turned slowly her way Celia's own eyes were shining suddenly with tears of joy, and without needing to ask she leaned in to touch the faded cheek with her own. 'Nevine!'

'And you . . . are Peter's daughter?' The embrace was emotional. Some time later, when eyes had been laughingly dried, Tariq's mother said, 'No one knows me as

Nevine now. From the days when I ceased to appear as a dancing girl my name has been Nadia. After your father left, my family were in despair for my reputation. But we are of Egyptian stock, a highly prized status in Bahraini society, and Tariq's father was persuaded to overlook my questionable past for the privilege of rearing fine, intelligent sons. We have a large family and he at least is content.'

There was no bitterness in Nevine's explanation, just smiling resignation, but Celia knew, just as she had known with her father, that the years had done nothing to extinguish the love that had been born between them so long ago, here in Bahrain.

'Of course Tariq knows nothing of my past,' Nevine added. 'That is something between my husband and me, and he has not spoken of it since the day of our marriage.'

Celia nodded absently. That would explain why nothing had come of her enquiries in these parts. But something else was on her mind. She repeated dreamily, 'No, Tariq knows nothing of your love for my father, but you and I know.' At the older woman's questioning look she rushed on, 'Don't you see? This alters everything! Tariq is your son. And I'm ... Peter's daughter. A match that couldn't take place thirty years ago can, in a way, do so now.

She stopped herself then, wondering at her impulsive proposition. Could she be happy here with Tariq, in the clamour and clutter of town life? Ironically these people had left the spaces and the desert behind, but she felt that something called to her out there, and it was all tied up with McCord in some way. But McCord was a businessman and he only had work plans, hadn't he? Trying to turn despair into practicality, she laughed harshly, 'What better way to link two people who never made it than to go ahead with this wedding now?'

Nevine didn't answer for a long moment. Celia felt that those searching dark eyes held a wisdom that saw

deep beyond one's smile. When she spoke her own smile
was gentle. 'I knew the moment I entered the room that
you were not in tune here, child, and you yourself
admitted it. Do you think a second unhappiness will
wipe out that of the past?' She rose. 'You must do as
you wish. If you marry Tariq I shall love you as the
daughter I consider you to be. But if you decide against
it all will be solved. It has been the wish of my husband
for some time to put Tariq in charge of the shipping
offices in Cairo and he has cousins and friends there
who will soon have him joining in their parties. I too
have a home there, so you see, after tonight, if this is
your choice, our paths will not cross again. The decision
is yours to make.'

She drew Celia into her arms, and after a long and
tense embrace when eyes of East and West were damp
again she turned and walked out of the room.

Celia stood around for a long while in a semi-trance,
and when the handmaidens came in to prepare her for
the wedding ceremony she did nothing to prevent it.
Later, in filmy gold-braided robes and headdress, alone
for a few moments before the attendants would come to
lead her to Tariq, she raised her eyes to the stars,
searching, hoping, but there was no mystic reply.

What there was was a distinct hammering on one of
the balcony doors.

Hardly had this registered on her mind than the glazed
parchment and latticework was splintering and shatter-
ing, giving way under the force of a great weight levelled
behind it. Standing there transfixed, Celia had the curious feeling that she had watched it all before.

When the door was matchwood and the debris scattered McCord said, stepping through the dust, 'Don't
think I'm going to spend the rest of our lives fishing
you out of these kind of crazy situations!'

Our lives! Celia felt a joyous pulsing rushing to her
head. She had forgotten all about the filmy raiment she
was wearing, and with his blue eyes whimsically ap-

praising McCord snapped, 'Put something on over that ridiculous get-up and let's get out of here.'

As overbearing as always! Unable to bring herself to obey meekly, Celia lifted her chin. 'There's something you don't understand. I've made an important discovery. Nevine is Tariq's mother. She's been here under our noses all the time ... and now that I've found her I've decided to join Tariq in a marriage that will make some amends for the past.'

'Over my dead body!'

Her carefully worded speech shot to pieces by his clipped comment, she said witheringly over a sneaking, soaring happiness, 'Do you have to be so melodramatic?'

'You pick these corny scenes, not me.' He swept her up in his arms and made for the outdoors.

The route down from the balcony round turrets and over ledges was painstakingly precarious, and gripped tight against McCord, Celia said with sarcasm, though she didn't raise her voice, 'Wouldn't it have been easier to knock at the front door and ask for Tariq?'

'I think I explained once before,' came the heavily breathing reply, 'that there's no talking to an Arab once he's made his mind up.'

They reached the ground and made for a path leading to the street. McCord looked back momentarily at the brightly lit household and growled, 'It took me one hell of a time to work out which room you were locked in.'

As there appeared to be no visible means of escape Celia asked testily, 'What are we going to do now?'

'I came in the Lamborghini,' McCord replied, unbuttoning his jacket, 'but that stays here now. Tariq will get the message when he knows I've delivered it back from my place.' With his off-white smile he draped the jacket round Celia. 'There's nothing for it but to take a taxi.'

'A taxi?' She was indignant. 'Like this?' But McCord

carted her off in his arms again, and later, when she was being bundled into the furry inside of a hired cab, she had to suffer the knowing looks of the winking Bahraini driver, and McCord's grin didn't do one thing to dispel the suggestion that she was being abducted against her will for some dark desert rendezvous.

She fumed all the way to El Zommorro, though below the paper-thin surface of her annoyance was a delicious, singing contentment.

It swelled within her as the undulating gardens and the desert house came into view, and he didn't let go of her until he had paid the man off and they were inside the rose-lit interior.

He had put her down in her favourite room where the chandelier winked over the dinner table set for two and the view through the open doorway of the palm-laden terrace was of a sky starlit and mystic in quality and desert stretches softened in the aura of night.

But there was nothing soft at the moment about McCord's attitude. Putting up with his grim surveillance where his jacket had slipped from her shoulders to the floor, Celia said pettishly, 'Well, don't just look at me as though I'm something the servants have forgotten to remove!'

'I happen to be looking at the world's prize idiot,' he barked, pacing. And levelling a finger at her in his old menacing way, 'Do you realise I've had to question the entire office staff to find out what happened to you? No one saw you leave. No one could tell me anything beyond when you were last seen. After fruitless enquiries in town I was left with the obvious conclusion that Tariq was behind your disappearance.'

Celia blinked, with a rosy glow in her heart. He had gone to all that trouble for her?

Still menacing, he went on, 'You've been a pain in the neck ever since I met you. I only gave you the job at the ice-rink to keep you out of trouble, and what did it get me? A whole load of trouble!'

'You could have sent me back to England,' she said guilelessly.

'That's beside the point,' he waved a hand brusquely. And sticking with his own line of thought, 'You've found a way to get under my skin at every turn.'

'Don't tell me your work hasn't been the same since I arrived?' Celia asked with gleeful innocence.

'That's putting it mildly,' he eased out a breath. 'That damnable defiance of yours has given me more headaches than any business deal.'

'And the party nights? Haven't they been the same either since I messed up your life?' Feeling deliciously malicious, she wanted him to keep making music in her ears.

'With you causing me endless sleepless nights, what good am I at a party?' He was moving in threateningly.

Celia sought to check him in mild panic with, 'If you hadn't been so overbearing maybe I wouldn't have rushed into Tariq's arms.'

'You would have gone anyway because you had to satisfy yourself that you'd got me in a spin.'

She mused over his words with pleasurable wonder. Could that have been why she did it? But on her guard again, she tossed at him, 'How could I suspect any such thing with you throwing Mandy at my head at every opportunity?'

'I had to do something to cut you down to size.' The ghost of a grin tugged at his mouth. 'You were so full of Tariq I reckoned a bit of outside competition would take some of the wind out of your sails.'

'Oh yes?' Celia ached to be convinced. 'Well, I saw the way you looked at Mandy that night of her solo spot on the ice.'

'Oh, you did?' Something twitched at his lips and his gaze had become slightly quizzical. 'And is it the same way I'm looking at you now?'

Celia was moved by an overwhelming tenderness in his eyes and every part of her being answering that deep emotion she replied with a dash of mischief, 'You're looking at me with the possessive eye of some desert sheikh.'

'Quite right,' he nodded. 'I played one for a while in abducting you here away from the distractions of the ice-rink.'

She eyed him with mock severity. 'And you made out it was for the purposes of work.'

'So it is in a way.' He pulled her into his arms. 'You're going to have your work cut out crossing me in my own house.'

'Are you going to be here?' She looked at him archly. 'Don't tell me you're thinking of relegating most of your work to other capable hands?'

'What do you think I've been doing all these weeks?' His arms were crushing her. 'I've got to have peace of mind somewhere.'

The song inside Celia trilled to a final, piercingly lovely note. Was *she* going to be his peace of mind!

Recapping, she said dreamily, 'Whatever gave you the idea that I should want to cross you?'

Finding her soft and pliable in his arms, McCord murmured, 'At the moment I can't think of a thing.' He sought her lips with a hunger that was devastating, but sweetly so, for with the same urgent need Celia clung to him, letting the tide of his love wash over her now, all-conquering, as she had always known it would be.

His mouth pausing briefly away from hers, he smiled hoarsely, 'You and I should get married right away, Miss Darwell.'

Celia raised her lips for more and said demurely, 'I'm in accord, Mr McCord.'

THE TALENTED SONJA HENIE

Two of Roumelia Lane's characters in *Desert Haven* are figure skaters—in particular Mandy Bennett, a world-class competitor. We thought our readers might be interested to learn about a real world-class skater from another era—Sonja Henie.

Born in Oslo, Norway, in 1913, Sonja learned to skate almost before she could walk. By the age of six she persistently tagged along after her older brother whenever he visited the local ice rink. By the time she reached her twenties this remarkable skater had amassed a string of championships that have made her, on record, the greatest female figure skater to date.

As the Olympic gold medalist in 1928, 1932 and 1936, title holder of the world amateur championship for ten consecutive years and national champion in her beloved Norway for even more years, it was no wonder that the young and pretty Sonja, in her dazzling skating costumes, was adored by crowds all over the world, presented to royalty—and frequently linked romantically with wealthy eligible bachelors!

She did get married—twice—to American citizens, but her colorful active life ended tragically in a plane crash in 1969. Despite her untimely death, Sonja's accomplishments had already earned her a place in history. It is to Sonja that we owe the graceful ballet movements of figure skating today—a dramatic improvement from the early days when skaters merely leaped from one stunt to another.

When Sonja finally retired from amateur skating after her heady Olympic triumph in 1936, she embarked on a new career of touring with spectacular ice shows and starring in Hollywood movies. Putting an ice star on film was a daring idea, but one that became an instant box-office hit. Best remembered in *Sun Valley Serenade*, Sonja played the girl next door who was also—what else—a figure skater. And in the fashion of Harlequin romances, by the time the curtain came down Sonja had won her man!